S0-ASK-923

14

Leave of Absence

Also by Tom Milton
Outside the Gate
The Golden Door
Sara's Laughter
A Shower of Roses
Infamy
All the Flowers
The Admiral's Daughter
No Way to Peace

Leave of Absence

Tom Milton

NEPPERHAN PRESS, LLC
YONKERS, NY

Copyright © Tom Milton, 2014

All rights reserved. No part of this book may be reproduced
or transmitted in any form or by any means, electronic or mechanical,
including photocopying, recording, or by any information storage
and retrieval system, without written permission from the author,
except for the inclusion of brief quotations in a review.

Published by Nepperhan Press, LLC
P.O. Box 1448, Yonkers, NY 10702
nepperhan@optonline.net
nepperhan.com

PUBLISHER'S NOTE
This is a work of fiction. Names, characters, places, and incidents
are the product of the author's imagination or are used fictitiously,
and any resemblance to actual persons, living or dead, events, or
locales is entirely coincidental.

Printed in the United States of America

Library of Congress Control Number: 2014902806

ISBN 978-0-9899571-1-3

Cover art was licensed from Publitek, Inc.

For Marie

Sin is refusing to love.

Fr. Carlos Mugica

Puerto Plata, 1999

ONE

WHEN THE TAXI drove away, Ronan was left alone on the dimly lit street with his luggage on the sidewalk, already wondering if it had been a good idea to come here.

Up and down the street there was no sign of life except in the building that he stood in front of. A dingy neon light above the entry said: "Hotel." To the right of the entry was a brighter light for what was evidently the main attraction: "Mike's Bar & Grill." Since at this point Ronan had no alternative, and since he trusted the person who had recommended this place, he picked up his bags and entered the building.

It had no lobby, and he found himself in a room that had tables where no one was seated and a quadrangular bar around which a diverse collection of guys was gathered. They looked like fugitives from the ends of the earth, and Ronan immediately felt at home among them.

As he approached the bar carrying his luggage a broad-backed guy in a faded yellow tee shirt turned around and greeted him in a language that he didn't understand.

"You speak English?" a guy in an army shirt asked.

"Yes," Ronan said. "I also speak Spanish."

"Are you looking for a room?" the guy behind the bar asked. He could have been a bartender in any Irish bar in New York, except that instead of letting you know he only worked there his manner let you know he owned the place.

"I am. Do you have one?"

"Sure I do. It's twenty a night."

"He means dollars, not pesos," the guy in the army shirt said.

"That's fine." Ronan dug into his pocket with the intention of paying in advance.

"You don't have to pay me now," the guy behind the bar said. "I trust you. Are you Irish?"

"Bronx Irish."

"Me too. I'm Mike."

"I'm Ronan." He reached across the bar between two guys, who graciously opened a passage for his arm, and shook hands with Mike.

"You want to see the room now or have a drink?"

"I'll have a drink."

"Sit down," a guy with frizzy blond hair and a ring in his ear said, patting a barstool.

Ronan set his luggage down on the floor and sidled to the bar.

"What'll you have?" Mike asked him.

"What kind of beer do you have?"

"There's only one kind of beer to drink in the Dominican Republic, and that's Presidente."

"I prefer Quisqueya," a guy across the bar said.

"You can have it. You don't know beer."

"I'll have a Presidente," Ronan said, taking Mike's advice.

"I'm Donal," the guy with the frizzy blond hair said. "What brings you to Puerto Plata?"

"I'm here on vacation."

Donal smiled indulgently. "That's what we all say. But people who come here on vacation don't come to this hotel. They go to the hotels on the beaches."

"Maybe he doesn't like beaches," another guy said.

"I don't like beaches," Ronan said. "I don't tan, I burn."

"You mean from the sun?" Donal asked.

"What else would burn you on a beach?" the other guy said.

"Flames from hell," Donal suggested.

"Flames from hell would never find you on a beach."

"They could find you anywhere."

"Anywhere except here," Mike said, setting a green bottle in front of Ronan. A folded paper napkin was wrapped around the neck of the bottle and pushed into the opening.

Ronan removed the napkin and took a swig. It tasted good. Though an overhead fan stirred the air above the bar, it was still hotter than it had been that day in New York, where they were having a heat wave.

Donal leaned toward him and said in a low confidential voice: "You see these guys around the bar? They're wanted by the law in their countries."

"How do you know?"

"I've heard their stories."

"Where are they from?"

"They're mostly from Europe. But that guy over there," Donal said, indicating the guy in the army shirt, "he's an American."

Ronan discreetly looked at the guy, who was chatting amiably with the guy in the yellow tee shirt. It sounded like they were speaking English, but he couldn't tell.

"There aren't many Americans here. They come as tourists, but they don't stay."

"Where are you from?" Ronan asked.

"I'm from Ireland. I'm wanted there for robbery."

"What did you steal?"

"An airplane."

"You're kidding."

"No. I'm a pilot. I was working for a rich bloke, flying his private plane, and one day I had an urge to fly off into the blue."

"Where did you go?"

"To Africa. And from there I flew to the Caribbean. I left the plane in Tortola, and I came here by boat. That was two years ago, and they still have no idea where I am."

"So what do you live on?"

"I fly a plane for someone every now and then. I don't need much. You can live on almost nothing here."

Before Ronan could comment the lights went off, and it was suddenly pitch dark. If he hadn't been grasping the bottle of beer he would have had trouble finding it.

"There they go again," a voice said.

"They must have switched the power over to Santiago."

"Or else a bird flew into a wire and shorted it out."

3

Within a few minutes Mike turned on a flashlight and headed for a back room.

"Does this happen often?" Ronan asked.

"It happens two or three times a day," Donal said.

"This afternoon it was out for three hours," a voice from across the bar said.

"That's nothing," another voice said. "The day before yesterday it was out for so long that the beer in my fridge wasn't cold anymore."

"You should have drunk the beer while it was still cold."

"I tried, but I couldn't drink it fast enough."

"How much beer did you have in your fridge?"

"As much as it'll hold. I use my fridge only for beer."

"What's the problem with the electricity?" Ronan asked.

"You don't want to hear the whole story," Donal told him, "so I'll give you a short version. The government distributes the electricity, which they buy from private power plants. The rich people don't pay for electricity because they can get away with it, and the poor people don't pay for it because they can always steal it by connecting their wires to the lines."

"Why doesn't the government cut off people who don't pay?"

"They're afraid to cut off the rich people, and they can't stop the poor people from reconnecting to the lines, so they don't collect enough money to pay the power plants. When the power plants don't get paid, they respond by reducing production, and that forces the government to ration electricity."

"And when they ration electricity, you can guess who gets it," the voice from across the bar said.

"The people in Santiago get it," another voice said. "They have more votes than the people here."

"When they built the new power plant in the harbor," Donal said, "they told us it would guarantee electricity for Puerto Plata, but it all goes to Santiago."

"We don't get a drop of it."

"You don't get drops of electricity."

"Then we don't get a volt of it."

At that moment the lights went on, accompanied by the muffled noise of a combustion engine.

"That's the generator," Donal said. "Without a generator you can't operate a business."

"You can't keep beer cold," the guy who used his refrigerator only for beer said.

After drinking another beer Ronan began to succumb to traveler's fatigue, and he asked Mike to show him the room.

He followed Mike up a stairway and down a hall and into a room, where Mike flicked on an overhead light. There was a bed with a mosquito net hanging over it, a chest of drawers, and a single chair.

"The rooms are small," Mike admitted, "but my girls do a good job of keeping them clean. You'll find the bathroom at the end of the hall."

"It looks fine," Ronan said, having slept in worse places.

"You should keep the windows open for air, but make sure the net is tight around the bed. If you don't, those critters will eat you alive. They love Irish skin."

"I will. Thanks."

"I open for breakfast at seven in the morning, and I serve it till four in the afternoon. So you can sleep as late as you want."

"That's good. I don't feel like getting up early."

"Sleep well," Mike said gently.

"Thanks," Ronan said.

Alone, he unzipped the bag in which he had packed his toiletries. He found his toothbrush and the tube of toothpaste, which he took down the hall to the bathroom. It was barely large enough to contain a shower, but it was clean, and all he had to do was relieve himself from drinking the beer and brush his teeth.

Back in the bedroom he unbuttoned his shirt and hung it on a plastic hanger in the open area for clothes, which consisted of a shelf and a plastic pole. He assumed that they used plastic because in this climate a metal hanger would corrode and a wooden pole would be eaten by insects. While hanging his pants he heard the air-raid siren of a mosquito, which he allowed to land on his forearm so that he could slap it.

Then, before another attacker could follow him, he turned off the light and entered the tent of the mosquito net and lay down.

Through the window came a soft light, presumably from the moon since the town was still without electricity, as evidenced by the hum of the generator, and in that light he could make out the features of the room. It could have been a monk's cell, except that there were no religious objects on the walls—no crucifix, no painting of a saint. And he felt at home in the bare room, just as he had felt at home among the fugitives at the bar.

Lying under what looked like a shroud in the moonlight, he felt that he was free. He was in a place where no one knew him and no one could find him since the only person who knew where he was would never betray his secret. His family knew he was on a leave of absence, and they knew he had left New York, but they didn't know where he had gone, and they didn't need to know, so they hadn't pressed him. They didn't understand why he was having a crisis, but they understood that he had to get away from his situation.

He was jolted by the sound of a jet plane flying low over the hotel. He expected to hear a crash, but the sound continued as if one plane after another was flying over. It made no sense for a fleet of planes to attack Puerto Plata, a provincial city in a country that wasn't at war with anyone, and as he sat up and listened further, careful not to disturb the mosquito net, he realized that the sound wasn't coming from planes but from a fixed position not far away.

After a half hour or so the sound finally stopped, and the city was quiet. In fact, it was quiet enough for Ronan to hear the siren of a mosquito on the other side of the net, trying to find a way through it to the warmth that offered a feast of blood.

He slept until after ten the next morning, and he took a shower in the bathroom down the hall, surprised and pleased that there was hot water.

Downstairs, he found Mike behind the bar and two guys whom he recognized from the night before sitting at the bar and drinking what looked like Bloody Marys. At a table two women in bright dresses were having coffee.

"*Buenos días,*" Mike said. "Did you sleep well?"

"Oh, yeah," Ronan said, sitting at the bar. "But just before I went to sleep there was a sound like jet planes flying low over the hotel."

Mike laughed. "That was the power plant in the harbor. It uses steam turbines to generate electricity, and once a day they flush out the turbines."

"It does sound like jet planes," the guy in the army shirt said. "The first time I heard it, I thought a plane was coming down."

"A plane came down a few years ago," the other guy said. "It landed in the ocean."

"Why are they allowed to do that?" Ronan asked.

The guys all laughed.

"They're allowed to do whatever they want," Mike said, "as long as they pay the right people in the government."

"And they know all the right people," the guy in the army shirt said.

"Who owns the plant?" Ronan asked.

"A company named Enron," the other guy said. "I think it's an American company."

"It is," Ronan said, remembering how his father had praised it.

"The sound is bad enough," the guy in the army shirt said. "But the smoke is even worse. If it blows your way, you can't breathe."

"That plant drove away a lot of tourist business," Mike said. "We used to have cruise ships in the harbor. People came into town and shopped. And they came here to eat."

"They came for your bacon-lettuce-and-tomato sandwiches," the other guy said.

"The prevailing wind," the guy in the army shirt said, "blows the smoke toward Santa Cruz. It usually goes into the *barrio*, but at times it rises and hides Cristo."

7

"Cristo?" Ronan asked, not understanding.

"You never heard of Jesus Christ?" the other guy teased him.

"It's a statue of Christ the Redeemer on top of the mountain," Mike said, rescuing him.

"Just like in Rio," the guy in the army shirt said.

"You been to Rio?" the other guy asked.

"No. But I've seen pictures of it."

"You can go to the top in the *teleférico*," Mike said.

"You mean when the *teleférico* is working," the guy in the army shirt said.

"It usually isn't working," the other guy said.

"I'd hate to be halfway up to the top and have an outage."

"They have their own generator."

"I wouldn't bet on it."

"If you make it to the top," Mike said, "you have a great view. You can see the whole city, and the beaches, and the other mountains."

"How far away is it?" Ronan asked.

"Twenty minutes. You can take a taxi there."

"Is it near the town of Santa Cruz?"

"The town is right under that mountain."

"Well, someone told me it was a good place to live."

"Are you planning to stay here for a while?"

Ronan shrugged. "Yeah, maybe."

"You can rent an apartment there by the month. It's off season, so you can get a good deal."

"Do you know anyone who can help me find an apartment?"

"Sure." Mike reached for his cell phone. He dialed a number and waited for a moment. "Janos? It's Mike. I have a guy here who needs an apartment. Yeah, he is. So if he goes to Santa Cruz in about an hour, where can he find you?"

Ronan sipped his coffee as Mike made a note on a napkin.

"Great. He'll look for you there." Mike turned off his phone and handed the napkin to Ronan, saying: "Just tell the taxi driver to go to this place."

"Thanks," Ronan said, reading the note. It said: "Las Palmas."

"Now, what would you like for breakfast?"

"What do you have?"

"I have eggs, bacon, home fries, and toast, just like any diner in New York."

"I'll have that, with the eggs scrambled, please."

Mike went through a doorway behind him, evidently into the kitchen.

"Santa Cruz is a nice town," the guy in the army shirt said. "There's a great place to drink on the beach. It's owned by a Dutch guy."

"His name is Joop," the other guy said.

"What's the name of the place?" Ronan asked.

The two guys looked at each other as if they didn't know.

"I think it's Joop's Beach Bar," the guy in the army shirt said.

"They have a round table there," the other guy said, "where people sit and drink all day."

"It's like here, except it's on the beach."

"He has good food there. They say he was a cook."

Remembering what Donal had said about the European residents, Ronan wondered what Joop was wanted for in his country.

After paying Mike and thanking him for everything, Ronan walked to the central plaza to find a taxi. It was a traditional Spanish-style plaza with old tropical trees in the middle and a tile walk around it. Before he reached the side where the taxis were parked he was accosted by a guy who offered to take him to the amber museum and by a pair of boys who offered to shine his shoes. He yielded to the boys, who had successfully tugged at his heart. They worked together on his shoes while he sat on a bench and watched them. They were six or seven, and he wanted to believe they weren't in school only because it was Saturday.

"Are you from New York?" one of them asked, tenderly rubbing cream into the leather.

"Yes. I am. How did you guess?"

"You look like an American. Do you know Alfonso Soriano?"

"I don't know him, but I've seen him play."

"He's a Dominican. He's from San Pedro de Macorís."

"I know," Ronan said. "There are a lot of Dominicans in *las grandes ligas.*"

The boys smiled as if his knowing there were a lot of Dominicans in major-league baseball made them happy.

He paid the boys, tipping them generously, and he hired the taxi at the head of the line and asked the driver to take him to Las Palmas in Santa Cruz.

The guy drove as if he valued his car, letting the motorbikes swarm around him.

There was a traffic light at the first major intersection they came to, but the light didn't work, so people drove through from all directions as if they were happy not to be restrained by this alien mechanism to control their behavior.

Along the main road were all kinds of small stores with people walking by them and standing in front of them, pausing to look at merchandise or to chat with someone.

As they were leaving town Ronan noticed a sign for the *teleférico*, and he asked the driver: "Is the *teleférico* working now?"

"Yes," the driver said. "But it's not a good time to go up there now. At this time of day there are clouds around the top of the mountain."

"What's a good time to go up there?"

"Early in the morning."

He expected the driver to offer to pick him up the next morning and take him to the *teleférico*, but the guy just kept driving carefully.

The road into Santa Cruz went through a wetland, and though it had been paved, it had a rough surface and major pot holes, which the driver skillfully maneuvered around. At one point they had to ford a stream.

Then, on both sides of the road, there were warrens of varicolored shacks with corrugated metal roofs. In the streets there were women carrying buckets of water or balancing parcels on their heads. And down a narrow lane two girls were strolling hand in hand.

"This is the *barrio*," the driver said as if he was giving a tour. "It's where the poor people live."

"Are there a lot of poor people in this town?" Ronan asked.

"Yeah, there are. They come here from the *campo*."

"Do they have a school?"

"Of course they have a school," the driver said. "It's in the middle of town. They have floods in the *barrio*, so you wouldn't put the school here."

"Why do they have floods?"

"Remember that bridge we crossed just before we turned onto this road? Well, that goes over the San Marco River, which floods during the rainy season."

"Does it flood every year?"

"Almost every year."

"Then why don't they control the floods?"

The driver gave him a look through the rear view mirror. "You know how I can tell you're not from here? You ask that kind of question."

"Okay. They don't have the money."

"That's right. But even if they had the money, they wouldn't use it for that purpose."

"What would they use it for?"

"What do you think?"

"To line their pockets."

"Now you're talking like you're from here—except for the accent. Are you from Colombia?"

"I lived there for a while, but I'm from New York."

"You sound like you're from Colombia."

"How do you know what people from Colombia sound like?"

"I was the driver for a businessman from Colombia. I had that job for almost three years, so I know what people from Colombia sound like."

"What business was he in?"

"Bras. He had a factory in the Zona Franca."

"I guess it was cheaper to make them in this country than in Colombia."

11

"I guess it was. But now it's cheaper to make them in China, so the factory's gone."

"Did people from the *barrio* work there?"

"Yes. They worked in all the factories in the Zona Franca, mostly sewing. But there aren't any factories left there now."

By now the taxi had climbed a hill and they were now on a plateau, where the buildings were made of cinder block, plastered over and mostly painted white, with terra cotta roofs. The street was lined with shops, including restaurants.

"The school is down that road to the left," the driver said.

The street ran into a plaza on which there was a church in the mission style. Across from the church was a building that looked like a town hall.

After leaving the plaza they climbed a ridge, where the houses were larger.

"This is where the rich people live," the driver said.

"Is Las Palmas for rich people?" Ronan asked, troubled.

"Oh, no. It's for tourists," the driver assured him. "And for people who need a place to live while they decide whether to stay here or go home."

They stopped in front of a three-story building, and the driver helped him get his bags out of the trunk. The driver seemed to appreciate the tip and gave him a card in case he needed a taxi again. His first name was Wilson.

A few minutes after the taxi pulled away a stocky guy who walked as if he were on a rolling ship came out of the building. He had sandy hair that was combed straight back from his high forehead and canny grey eyes.

"Are you Ronan?"

"Yes. Are you Janos?"

"I am," Janos said, extending his hand. He spoke English with an accent that sounded Eastern European. "So you need a place to live for a while."

"Do you have an apartment available?"

"I have an apartment in this building. Your timing is good. I just evicted the previous tenants for not paying the rent. I'll show it to you."

He followed Janos into the building and up the stairs.

"It's on the third floor," Janos said, "but it's worth the climb. It has a great view."

"I don't mind the stairs," Ronan said.

They went into a furnished apartment that had wide windows through which you could see the beach and the ocean beyond it. Approaching a window, Ronan looked down on the terra cotta roofs of the houses between the building and the beach. He noticed a woman in a courtyard hanging clothes up to dry.

"From the balcony you can see the mountain," Janos said, leading him out there.

On the balcony was a small plastic table with two plastic chairs, suggesting that the previous tenants had been a couple. Ronan looked away from the ocean and saw the mountain looming above them. Its wooded side was darkened by shadow and its top was surrounded by gray clouds, so while you could see the lines of the *teleférico* rising and gradually disappearing into the mist, you couldn't see the statue of Christ the Redeemer.

"What's the rent?" Ronan asked.

"We're off season," Janos said, "so the rent is only two hundred a month. It's two hundred through December, and then it's three hundred from January through April."

"That's fine. Do you accept cash?"

Janos smiled. "It's the only thing I do accept. There are people who come here under false identities, with stolen credit cards. I've learned from my mistakes."

"I wish I could say that," Ronan almost said.

They went back inside, where Janos took a piece of paper out of his pocket and handed it to Ronan. "This is the lease. It gives both parties the right to cancel with thirty days' notice."

"That sounds fair." After verifying that the rent was two hundred dollars a month, Ronan took the pen that was offered him and signed the lease without reading further.

"I'll make a copy of this for you. I mean, when the power goes back on."

"Does the building have a generator?"

"No. If it did, the rent would be higher. It's peaceful without the noise of a generator. At night you can hear the surf."

"I just wondered. I don't need electricity."

"You mean you can live without a computer?"

"I can live without lights as long as I have candles."

"You can buy candles at the local store. It has everything."

"How far is the store from here?"

"It's a short walk. It's on the main road, this side of the plaza. It's called Nelly's."

When Janos had left him, Ronan unpacked and put away his clothes. He had brought only summer clothes and only enough underwear for a week without having to do laundry. That had enabled him to travel light.

The kitchen area had a stove, a refrigerator, and cabinets that contained everything he would need for cooking and eating and drinking. He only had to buy some food and beverages.

Using the pen and the notebook he had brought, he made a shopping list, and then he left the apartment and descended the stairs. About halfway down he caught a whiff of onions cooking, which made him think about having lunch, and he decided to find a place to eat before he went to Nelly's.

On the way to the main street he passed a taxi stand where several cars were parked and the drivers were playing dominoes. The guy who had driven him from Puerto Plata wasn't among them, presumably having returned to his own base.

The main street had a lot of traffic, mostly motorbikes, which zoomed by like fighter planes. There was often a passenger on the bike, and sometimes there were several passengers—a pair of girls, a mother and a child, a whole family. Ronan didn't want to think about what would happen to the passengers if the bike hit one of those potholes.

Across from Nelly's was a restaurant called Solo Chivo, which meant "only goat." He liked goat, though he couldn't believe that a restaurant would serve only goat. Since there were people at the tables, he walked in and sat down where the proprietor indicated. The tables were in the open air, under a roof of palm fronds.

A waiter came and asked him what he would like to drink, and since he was thirsty from his walk, he ordered a Presidente and asked: "How's the goat?"

"*Es muy rico*," the waiter said. "It's our specialty."

"Do you serve things other than goat?"

"Oh, yes. We have sandwiches and pasta, whatever you want."

"I'll have the goat. What does it come with?"

"*Habichuelas y arroz blanco.*"

"That sounds perfect."

The waiter brought him a green bottle with a folded paper napkin wrapped around its neck.

As he drank the beer Ronan watched the traffic going by— the pedestrians, the motorbikes, the trucks, and the cars. Like everywhere else, the class structure was reflected by the mode of transportation, with people who walked at the bottom and people who drove expensive vehicles at the top. In the latter he noticed a few white faces.

The food tasted even better than it did back home at the Dominican restaurant where he went frequently, maybe because he was eating in the open air.

He paid the waiter and walked across the street to Nelly's, stopping at the entrance to pick up *Hoy* and putting the newspaper into a red plastic shopping basket. The store was packed with food and beverages and household items, and the aisles were so narrow that you had to step aside to let another person pass. He explored the store and noted items to buy later, and then he started looking for items on his list.

He was standing in front of the cardboard containers of juices when a young woman with coffee-colored skin came into the aisle. She was dressed professionally in a tailored light blue shirt with three-quarter sleeves and khaki pants, which weren't tight-fitting like the jeans that most of the girls wore. Her dark hair was clamped back in a pony tail, and her dark eyes were serious. Around her neck was a fine gold chain, at the end of which hung a gold cross.

15

He stepped aside to let her pass, but she stopped next to him and looked up at the top shelf.

"I'm sorry to trouble you," she said in English, "but could you reach up and get me a roll of paper towels? I pulled a muscle in my back, and it kills me to reach up."

"Sure," he said, happy to help her. "Do you want Bounty?"

"No, thanks. I'll take the local brand."

He reached up and got a roll and handed it to her.

"Thanks," she said, taking it.

For a moment they were close enough together so that he could smell the floral scent of her perfume, and then she moved away, going down the aisle. With her upright posture she had a bearing that radiated confidence and self-respect.

Standing still in admiration, he followed her with his eyes until she disappeared around the corner of the aisle.

By the time he reached the checkout counter she was gone.

He carried his groceries back to his apartment, a plastic bag in each hand. Along the way a guy on a motorbike stopped and offered him a ride, which he politely declined.

When he had put everything away he opened the bottle of rum he had bought and poured some into a glass. He went out to the balcony and sat down in one of the chairs and enjoyed the view of the beach and the ocean, sipping the rum.

Then he turned to look up at the mountain. The clouds had parted, and towering above him, resplendent in the sunlight, was Christ the Redeemer with arms spread in a gesture of forgiveness that included everyone, even him.

TWO

THE NEXT MORNING Ronan had breakfast on the balcony with his back to the mountain, facing the ocean. The beach was close enough so that if he had known them he could have recognized the people walking along it. A white woman, whom he could have seen driving by Solo Chivo in one of those expensive cars, was walking a white dog like the kind you would see on upper Madison Avenue. A couple, who acted as if they were newly in love, ambled along with arms wrapped around each other. Some boys were playing a game with a ball.

At the store he had bought a local coffee called Santo Domingo, a freshly baked loaf of sourdough bread, and butter from Sosua. He had hoped to find mangos but they were evidently out of season, so he had settled for a papaya, a piece of which he had skinned and sprinkled with lime juice. It all tasted good, and as he sipped the remainder of his coffee he read the sections of *Hoy* that he hadn't gotten to last evening since the sun had gone down not long after seven and the power hadn't come on until early morning.

In particular he read the sports section, which had broad coverage of baseball since there were Dominicans playing on virtually every major league team. The main interest in all the stories was how the Dominicans had performed, so the lead sentence of the story about the Yankees game was that Soriano had made a two-out RBI in the bottom of the second inning as well as participating in two double plays. Of lesser interest was the fact that the Yankees had lost to the Blue Jays four to ten.

After finishing the sports section Ronan checked his watch and decided that it was time to walk to the church in the plaza

17

and find out when the masses were. He had intended to check the schedule of masses the previous day but for some reason it had slipped his mind. It was after ten now, but he figured there would be a mass at eleven or twelve, so he had plenty of time to attend one. For a while he had considered not going to church, but he had decided that in his situation he needed all the help he could get.

As he walked from the ridge down into the main street it got warmer, and he slowed his pace to the speed at which the locals moved. When they were walking, as opposed to driving cars or riding motorbikes, they were never in a hurry.

From across the plaza he could see that the church's door was open, and that people were going in, so he concluded that there was a mass at eleven.

He followed a woman with two small children and a baby in arms into the church, letting her continue ahead of him. Inside, the walls of the church were white and the windows were tinted brown, presumably to filter out the tropical sunlight. Behind the altar was a large crucifix carved out of dark wood.

The church was filling up, and the only remaining empty seats were in the front and in the back. Without stopping at the holy water, Ronan went to the left aisle and sat down at the end of the last pew, as far away from the altar as possible.

By the time the mass began he had to stand up and let a family go into the pew.

"*En el nombre del Padre, y del Hijo, y del Espíritu Santo,*" the priest said.

"Amen," the congregation said after making the sign of the cross.

The priest had an altar boy but no assistant, and Ronan wondered how he would administer Communion to such a large number of people.

When they came to the penitential rite he wished he was somewhere else, but he joined the congregation saying: "*Yo confieso ante Dios todopoderoso, y ante vosotros, hermanos, que he pecado mucho de pensamiento, palabra, obra y omisión.*"

After that it got easier, and he participated in the Gloria and listened closely to the readings. He had often attended masses in

Spanish, but for some reason this one seemed longer than any he remembered, even though it wasn't a high mass.

"*Cordero de Dios, que quitas el pecado del mundo, ten piedad de nosotros,*" he recited with the congregation while a baby cried from the other side of the center aisle.

As he moved up the line to receive Communion with his head bowed and his hands clasped in front of him, Ronan wondered if he was doing the right thing. He probably should have first gone to Confession, but it was too late now.

Beyond the person ahead of him, he saw the face of the woman he had helped in the store. She was helping the priest by serving as an extraordinary minister.

"*El Cuerpo de Cristo,*" she said solemnly, placing a host into his outstretched hands.

Turning from her, Ronan put the host into his mouth and blessed himself and walked back down the side aisle to the last pew, where he knelt and prayed for all the people he could think of and last of all for himself.

Since he was in the back of the church, he was one of the first to leave when the mass had ended, and since he didn't know anyone, he had no intention of lingering. But there in the light of day, as if she were waiting for him, the woman who had served as extraordinary minister was standing in his path. Today she was wearing a green tailored shirt.

"Hello," she said in English with a warm smile. "I'm glad to see you."

"You are? Why?" he almost said. But instead he said: "I'm glad to see you."

"My name is Daria," she said, extending her hand.

He shook her hand, saying: "I'm Ronan."

"You're new here. You must be an American."

"I guess you can tell from my accent."

"Yeah, and I guess you can tell from my accent that I'm from the Bronx."

Now that she had mentioned it, he did detect a Bronx accent,

19

but it was flavored with what he had come to recognize as a Latino accent. "I guess I can."

"Would you like to have lunch?" she asked him without formalities.

He hesitated. He hadn't intended to get involved with anyone, but he finally decided that she was only welcoming a new arrival. "Yeah. Sure."

"I was planning to go to a place on the beach. It's called Joop's Beach Bar."

"I've heard of it, but I haven't been there."

"Then I can introduce you to it."

He expected her to have a car, but she started walking back the way he had come, and he went along with her, asking: "Do you live near the beach?"

"No. I live in the *barrio* next to my clinic. I'm a doctor, a family practitioner with a specialty in pulmonology."

He was impressed. "Where did you study medicine?"

"At Albert Einstein. It's in the Bronx."

"I know. I'm from Yonkers."

"You are? I did my undergraduate in Yonkers."

"At St. Catherine?"

"How did you guess?"

"It's the only college in Yonkers besides Sarah Lawrence, and for some reason I didn't think you went there."

"I couldn't afford Sarah Lawrence," she said. "But I got a very good education at St. Catherine. I was accepted by all the medical schools I applied to."

He could have mentioned that he knew people at St. Catherine, but it might have opened up a part of his life that he didn't want to go into, so he dropped the subject.

"Are you on vacation?" Daria asked after a silence.

"Yeah, I'm a teacher. I'm off for the summer."

"Lucky you. Where do you teach?"

"At Sacred Heart in Yonkers."

"That's a good school. What made you come to Santa Cruz?"

"A friend recommended it." Wanting to direct the questions back at her, he asked: "How long have you had your clinic here?"

"It's almost four years. I did my residency at Montefiore, and then I worked at a clinic in the Bronx. I would have stayed there, but about five years ago I came here on vacation. I was born in Santa Cruz, and I came to visit my relatives."

"You were born here?"

"Yeah, I was born in the *barrio*. I left with my family and went to the Bronx when I was nine."

They had come to the taxi stand where the drivers were still playing dominoes.

"*Quién gana?*" Daria asked as if she knew them.

"Roberto's winning," one of them said. "He's on a hot streak."

"You came to visit your relatives," he prompted her as they took care not to alarm a mother chicken and her babies who were scratching for food at the edge of the road.

"Yeah, and while I was here I saw that the *barrio* needed a doctor, so I decided to build a clinic."

"You saw that the *barrio* needed a doctor, but did you have a particular mission?"

"I did," she said, turning onto a street called Guarocuya. "But instead of telling you about it, I'll show you after lunch. Okay?"

"Okay," he said, expecting a tour of the *barrio*.

They followed Guarocuya over the ridge and down to a road that ran along the beach. There were a lot of cars parked between the road and the sea grape trees, and there were a lot of people on the beach in family groups.

"Sunday is a big day at the beach," Daria explained. "They come from Puerto Plata and all the way from Santiago."

The sound of a *merengue* blasted from the back of a red pickup.

She led him through the sea grape trees, ducking under a low branch and weaving through the trunks with grace. She emerged in a clearing that was surrounded on three sides by trees, with the open side facing the ocean.

A guy slowly rose from a large round table at the back of the clearing and came to greet her. He had short hair that must have once been blond and deep lines in his leathery face that must have been etched by whatever had made him leave his country.

21

"*Hola, mi amor,*" he said to Daria, bowing slightly.

"*Hola, señor,*" she replied to him. "I've brought a new arrival."

"It's a pleasure," the guy said, extending his hand to Ronan. "I'm Joop."

"I'm Ronan. I've heard a lot about you."

"Whatever you heard from that guy over there," Joop said, gesturing toward the table, "it's not true. So don't believe it."

Donal was sitting at the table, drinking a beer.

"Donal's a gossip," Daria said, agreeing with Joop, "so don't tell him anything unless you want the whole world to know it."

"I have nothing to tell," Ronan said.

"Well, if you do have anything," Joop said, "you can safely tell it to Daria. She won't reveal your deepest secrets. In that respect she's like a priest."

"I'm not like a priest. I'm only a doctor."

"Then I take that back. You're not like a priest. You're really like a saint."

Ignoring his praise, Daria asked: "What are your specials for lunch today?"

"I have stewed goat and free-range chicken."

"Like the chickens we saw at the edge of the road?"

"I bought the chicken. I paid good money for it."

"I know you did," Daria said, poking him affectionately. "Come on, Ronan. Let's take the table over there. I want to smell the ocean."

Before they could move, a German shepherd came over to greet Daria, wagging his tail and nuzzling her, and to check out Ronan, sniffing him.

"Hi, Gunter," she said, petting the dog.

When they sat down in the white plastic chairs at the white plastic table, Daria kicked her shoes off and buried her toes in the fine sand. With her eyes closed, she inhaled deeply and then exhaled slowly.

"Ah," she murmured. "When I breathe this pure air I feel blessed."

"I can see why you like coming here," he said, gazing out at the endless ocean.

"All people have the right to breathe pure air. But many people are deprived of that right. Many people breathe air that makes them sick and kills them."

Before he could find out which people in particular she had in mind, a pretty girl in tight jeans came to wait on them.

"*Hola, doctora,*" the girl said with a friendly smile.

"*Hola, Katiuska. Como estás?*"

"*Muy bien. Y usted?*"

"*Estoy muy feliz porque tengo un neuvo amigo. Se llama Ronan.*"

"*Mucho gusto, señor,*" the girl said respectfully.

"*Mucho gusto, señorita,*" Ronan said.

"What would you like to drink?" Daria asked him.

"I'll have a Presidente."

"*Dos Presidentes.*"

"*A sus ordenes.*"

"What a nice girl," Ronan said after she had left them.

"How old do you think she is?"

"I don't know. Sixteen?"

"She's fifteen. She was raised in captivity. They snatched her from a street in the *barrio* when she was twelve and made her a sex slave."

"Oh, my God. That happens here?"

"It happens everywhere. There are millions of girls—and boys—in sex slavery."

"How did she escape from it?"

"My friend Filomena rescued her. Now she has a home, she goes to school, and she has a job here on weekends."

"What happened to her parents?"

"We don't know what happened to them."

"So the girl lives with foster parents?"

"She lives with Filomena," Daria said, "along with nineteen other kids."

"You mean kids that your friend rescued?"

"That's right. If we have a saint here, it's Filomena."

The girl returned with two green bottles, their necks wrapped as usual with paper napkins.

"I'll have the chicken," Daria said.

"I will too," Ronan said. "I had goat yesterday."

"*Muy bien, señores,*" Katiuska said before going off.

"Where did she get the name Katiuska? It's a Polish name."

"She got it from a list of names that Filomena has. The girls always take new names when they go to live with her. It helps to give them new identities."

"Maybe I should take a new name."

"You want a new identity?" Daria asked, tilting her head and looking at him with curiosity.

"Maybe," Ronan said. "*No estoy contento con my identidad actual.*"

"Where did you learn to speak Spanish so well?"

"In Colombia. I spent three years there."

"What were you doing there?"

"I was building schools."

"Where did you learn how to build schools?"

"I worked for my father's construction company during the summers while I was in college."

"Your father owned a construction company? You must have lived in a nice area."

"I lived near Sarah Lawrence. My family still lives there, but I live in South Yonkers now."

"I know that area. It's mostly Latino."

"I feel at home there."

"Well, if you feel at home there," Daria said, smiling, "you'll certainly feel at home here."

"I felt at home the moment I arrived here."

"Then maybe you'll stay beyond the summer."

"Maybe I will. The truth is, I'm on a leave of absence from the school."

"You mean a sabbatical?"

"It's the same thing."

"It's not the same thing. Sabbaticals are for people who earn them. Leaves of absence are for people who need them."

"I fall into the latter category."

"Since I just met you, I won't ask why you needed a leave."

"I'll tell you why I needed one. I had a crisis."

"What kind of crisis?"

"A career crisis."

"You mean you began to wonder if you were pursuing the right career?"

"Yeah, I began to have doubts about it."

"Did something happen?"

"Nothing happened," Ronan said. "And that was the problem. I felt that something *should* be happening."

Daria nodded as if she understood. "I used to feel that way at times, but I haven't since I found my mission."

"Then I need to find a mission."

"Well, maybe you can find one here in Santa Cruz."

At that point Katiuska returned with place settings and a tray of condiments that included ketchup, mustard, and steak sauce.

"*Cómo va la escuela de verano?*" Daria asked her.

"It's going well. I like my teachers."

"This gentleman is a teacher."

"You are? Where do you teach?"

"I teach at a high school in New York."

"It's a Catholic school like yours," Daria added.

"Are you a brother?" the girl asked innocently.

"No, I'm a lay teacher. Most of us now are lay teachers."

"I want to be a teacher," Katiuska said.

"You'll make a good one," Daria told her.

When the girl had left them Ronan said: "So the church supports the school here?"

"Yeah. The government doesn't have money for it. In fact, they don't have money for the schools in Puerto Plata. The schools there have three shifts per day."

"Three shifts per day?"

"One in the early morning, one in the middle of the day, and one in the evening. Each shift is barely four hours, so the kids don't spend much time in school."

"What about the kids here?"

"They're in school all day. And they go to summer school. It keeps them out of trouble."

"Where does the school get its funding?"

"From donors in this community and in New York."

"Do the teachers like working through the whole year?"

"They love it. And they make more money."

"You couldn't do that in New York."

"I know you couldn't. You can't do a lot of things in New York that you can do here."

Katiuska brought their food, and they began eating.

"This is great food," Ronan said.

"I heard that Joop was a chef in a restaurant in Amsterdam," Daria said. "But I didn't hear that directly from him, so I don't know if it's true."

"Well, he learned to cook somewhere. That's what matters."

When they had finished eating, Daria excused herself and got up and walked to a shack on the other side of the round table. She went into the shack and closed the door behind her.

Alone, he gazed at the beach, where a mother was teaching a boy to swim. She held him by the armpits while he flailed his arms and his legs in the water, making little white splashes and going nowhere.

On her way back from the shack, which evidently was the bathroom, Daria paused to banter with the guys at the round table. She seemed perfectly at ease with them, aware of the way they looked at her but neither minding their attention nor encouraging it. You could see that they had great respect for her, but that didn't stop them from having lustful thoughts about her.

"Who are those guys?" he asked her when she had sat down.

"They're fugitives," she said lightly.

"What are they fleeing from?"

"Responsibility. That doesn't make them bad people," she added. "They were bored with their lives back home, and they're here in this country looking for adventure."

"I heard they're wanted by the law in their countries."

Daria laughed. "Did you hear that from Donal?"

"Yeah, I did. You mean it's not true?"

"Well, maybe some of them *are* wanted by the law, but most of them are here just looking for adventure."

"What kind of adventure?"

Daria smiled leniently. "What other kind of adventure is there for middle-aged males?"

"Oh," he said, comprehending.

"Most of those guys have Dominican girlfriends. They usually don't bring them to the round table because they want to relax in male company."

"Do they have wives and children back home?"

"I assume they do. They're normal males." She drank the last of her coffee and asked: "Do you like to walk?"

"Sure," he said, willing to go anywhere with this woman.

"I want to show you something."

They split the check, and they walked along the beach road. By now there were cars parked between the road and the beach, and they were still coming. Ahead of them a pickup truck pulled in under a sea grape tree with a lot of kids in back—as soon as it stopped, they jumped out and raced toward the water.

Among the people enjoying the beach there were no apparent race or class distinctions. Awed by the prospect of the endless ocean, they acknowledged their common humanity.

Leaving the beach, they headed down a street that was lined with palm trees. On one side were large houses whose property extended to the beach, and on the other side were apartment buildings. One of these buildings actually looked like a hotel, with a grand entrance through the grille of which you could see a fountain in a Spanish-style courtyard. Over the gate in bronze letters was the name of the place: "Arabian Nights."

"Is that a hotel?" Ronan asked as they passed the gate.

"Yeah, it is," Daria said. "It's for sex tourism."

"What do you mean?"

"I mean it's for guys who want to have sex with young girls— and young boys."

"Where do they come from?"

"America, Canada, Europe, Japan."

"How young are the girls?"

"Some are in their teens, but some are only twelve, eleven, ten—" She stopped, leaving the clear impression that she could have kept going down in age.

"Is that legal?"

"No. But we're like every other country in the world. If you want to do something illegal, you only have to pay the right person."

"Who's the right person?"

"The governor, the mayor, the chief of police."

Ronan was beginning to see a pattern. "So the people who run this hotel can do anything they want?"

"Anything they want. This street isn't zoned for a hotel, let alone a hotel like that. But they paid someone and got a permit."

"The people who own houses on this street must not like it."

"They don't like it. And they have a lot of money. But they don't have as much money as the organization that runs this business."

"Is it like a drug cartel?"

"*Sí, lo es,*" Daria said. "The organizations that cater to human weaknesses are all the same. They have the money, and they control the world. Or they think they do."

"You think you can fight them?"

"I know I can. And I know I can win."

At the end of the street they turned into another street and began to climb a hill. It was a steep hill, and as Ronan kept up with Daria he realized that in spite of his efforts to stay in shape, he wasn't in as good shape as she was, but he tried not to show it.

They were almost at the top of the hill when he began to hear what sounded like a factory powered by steam. As they got closer to its source, the noise got louder.

"Is that the power plant?" he asked.

"Yes," she said. "You'll see it in a few minutes."

They were now on a street that ran along a high ridge. On their left was the green ocean below, and on their right was the dark mountain above them, with Christ the Redeemer on its peak, suddenly too close for comfort.

"This was a great location for a house," Daria said, raising her voice so that she could be heard above the noise. "These houses have a view of the ocean and a view of the mountain, and some of them have a view of the harbor."

"Except for the noise, it's a great location," he shouted back. He had noticed that the houses all had "For Sale" signs.

They stopped in front of a four-story building that no longer had windows or a roof. Its pink walls were faded from the sun and were being taken over by creeping foliage.

"This was the Harbor View Hotel," Daria said. "Tourists came here from all over the world. They had such a good time that they came back. But one year they came back and found that they couldn't hear each other talk in their rooms. And when they put their towels out to dry, they found them coated with soot."

"So they stopped coming."

"Yeah, and within a year the hotel went out of business. Directly or indirectly it employed more than two hundred people. It was the town's biggest employer."

Daria waved to an old guy in uniform who was sitting at the entrance with a shotgun, guarding what was left of the place, and then she walked on.

About a hundred feet beyond the hotel was an opening in the trees, and you could see the power plant down at the edge of the harbor. With its tanks and pipes, it looked like an oil refinery. The noise was evidently coming from a steam-powered turbine, and from where they stood it was deafening.

What struck him was the black smoke emitted by the chimney. It filled the air above the plant and flowed down into the *barrio*, whose features were obscured in a haze.

"That smoke must be polluting the air," Ronan said, stating the obvious.

"It's poisoning the air," Daria said. "It's loaded with sulfur dioxide, particulate matter, and nitrogen oxide, not to mention carbon dioxide. The plant burns a fuel oil that's cheap because

29

it's dirty. If you use that type of oil in rich countries you have to install filters or scrubbers, which cost a lot of money, so they don't use it much anymore."

"Is what they're doing legal in this country?"

"No. But it's like that hotel for sex tourism—if you want to do something illegal, you only have to pay the right person."

"And the smoke goes into the *barrio*."

"Yeah. The prevailing wind blows it there. The chimney is positioned so the smoke won't bother the rich people."

"How long ago did they build the plant?"

"They stared it in 1994 and they completed it a year later. But they didn't build it here. They brought it from another country and installed it here."

"How did they bring it?"

"They towed it on barges. They claimed it was a new plant with the latest technology, but it was actually a used plant from South Korea with outmoded technology. That's what we get in poor countries—used plants with outmoded technology."

"I heard it's owned by Enron."

"It is. Do you know anything about them?"

"I only know they're a hot company," Ronan said. He decided not to reveal the fact that his father had recently invested in the company's stock.

"Well, they're doing evil things. This plant caused the loss of more than two hundred jobs in our town, and it's causing serious health problems for people in the *barrio*."

"What kind of problems?"

"Chronic bronchitis and emphysema, which are forms of chronic obstructive pulmonary disease. The smoke also aggravates the condition of people who have asthma, and it decreases the birth weight of babies."

He now understood why as a young doctor with a specialty in pulmonology she had given up everything to come here. "Do you have a lot of patients with those problems?"

"I have hundreds of them."

"Can you cure them?"

"No. There's no cure for chronic obstructive pulmonary

disease. I can only treat them—and pray to God that I can make their shortened lives more bearable."

"What about the plant? Can't you stop it from polluting the air?"

"I've been trying to stop it. I have lawsuits in process, and whenever I have the opportunity I explain to politicians that the plant—which is owned by foreigners—is killing our people."

"How do they respond?" Ronan asked.

"They pretend to take me seriously," Daria muttered, "but they don't do anything about it."

"That must be very frustrating."

"At times I wonder if the only solution is to blow up the plant. I can understand why people resort to violence."

He didn't comment.

"We're not supposed to use violence, but maybe the just war doctrine would apply to this situation."

"The just war doctrine?"

"The doctrine that allows the use of violence under certain circumstances."

"Would it allow you to blow up the plant?"

"I don't know. I should ask the priest. But I don't want to blow up the plant. I just want them to tow it away, as they threaten to do when the government doesn't pay them."

"Why does the government owe them money?" Ronan asked, wanting to verify Donal's explanation.

"The government buys power from them and distributes it. But a lot of people don't pay for electricity, so the government doesn't have money to pay the plant, and when the plant runs out of money to pay for fuel, it shuts down."

"Is that why we have outages?"

"It's the main reason," Daria said. "Another reason is that they don't generate enough power to satisfy the need for it, so at peak times they ration it."

"If they don't generate enough power, then the country needs that plant."

"It does. But that doesn't justify what the plant is doing to people in the *barrio*. So they have to clean it up, or tow it away, or else—" She hesitated. "I'll have to take drastic action."

"How long are you willing to give them?"

"Well, every day the plant is killing people in the *barrio*, so I'm not willing to give them much longer."

"Then you better ask the priest if the just war doctrine would allow you to blow up the plant."

"I'll ask him tomorrow."

They stood for a while watching the smoke blow into the *barrio*, and then they left.

They parted where the road divided, with Daria heading toward the *barrio* and Ronan heading back to his apartment.

Descending the hill, he thought about their conversation. When she had said that at times she wondered if the only solution was to blow up the plant, she had been expressing a feeling, not an intention, though in bringing up the just war doctrine she seemed to want a justification for acting on that feeling. Yet it was hard for him to imagine her blowing up the plant. It was the kind of thing that terrorists did, and this admirable woman who served the *barrio* as a doctor and served the church as an extraordinary minister certainly wasn't a terrorist.

Still, after hearing what the smoke was doing to the people in the *barrio* he supposed that if all other efforts failed to stop the plant from polluting the air, then blowing it up would be morally justified—as long as no one was hurt by the violence.

He wondered what the priest would say.

THREE

THE NEXT MORNING, conscious of his trouble keeping up with Daria on their way up the hill to see the power plant, he began a program of regular exercise. In shorts and a tee shirt, with flip-flops on his feet, he went to the beach before breakfast, intending to take a long walk.

It was a few minutes after seven, and the rising sun was still below the roofs of the houses, providing only shafts of light through blocks of deep shadow. At home there would have been birds singing at this hour, but the only sound was the rustle of the waves breaking on the shore, subdued because the bay was protected by a coral reef.

As he walked along the beach road a dog joined him, no doubt in the hope that there would be food at their destination. Ronan had already seen a number of dogs like this one. It had a short tan coat and a body so lean that its rib bones showed, and its head proclaimed an ancestry of jackals, not wolves.

The dog kept pace with him, neither advancing ahead of him nor lagging behind him, as if to make sure that they got to their destination at the same time.

Looking ahead, he noticed that there were cars parked in front of Joop's. He would have expected to see Joop's car there at this hour since he opened the place at eight, but there were several cars, and as Ronan got closer he could read the word "Policía" on a white van.

When he got to the other side of the sea grape trees he saw a group of people on the beach that included two uniformed cops, standing around an unseen object of attention.

With the dog still tagging along, he approached the group.

About halfway there the dog stopped and began to whimper.

At that point a member of the group turned toward him. It was Daria in a sweatshirt and jeans, with her hair in a rough pony tail, looking as if she had been roused from sleep to deal with an emergency.

"What happened?" he asked.

"We have a dead girl," she said grimly.

He stopped, realizing that she didn't want him to get any closer. "Can I help?"

"No. And you don't want to see what happened to her."

He imagined that the girl had been attacked by a shark or by barracudas, so he really didn't want to see what had happened to her, but he felt a compulsion to see, and he advanced, saying: "I'm not squeamish."

"You're not? All right," Daria said, stepping aside.

Lying on the sand, in an ungainly position, was a girl in a flimsy yellow skirt. Her bleached hair was bedraggled, and her face was badly beaten. Around her throat were ugly purple bruises. Her flowered blouse was torn from the shoulder, revealing a tattoo—a heart with the word "Amor" in the middle.

"Oh, God," he said, dismayed by the scene.

"A guy who was jogging on the beach found her."

"Do you know who she was?"

"There was no identification on her," Daria said, "but one of the cops recognized her. He says she worked at Arabian Nights. He thinks she was killed there by a tourist, and her body was thrown into the ocean. It didn't go far."

"How old was she?"

"About twelve."

"Oh, God," he repeated.

In response to a command by a guy in plainclothes, the two cops gently lifted the body and laid it on a stretcher. The rest of the people watched as they carried the stretcher to the van, moving as if they were in a funeral procession.

Daria gazed after them with tears in her eyes.

"Can I buy you a coffee?" Ronan asked.

"Sure. I really need a shot of rum, but I'll settle for coffee."

They sat down at a table, joined by the dog that had come along with Ronan to the point where it had smelled death. It lay down under the table, positioning itself for the possibility of food being dropped or offered.

After a few minutes Joop came over to serve them, walking stiffly as if he was in pain.

"How are you doing?" Daria asked him.

"Not so well," Joop said. "That wasn't such a good way to begin the day."

"It certainly wasn't. Did you ever see that girl before?"

"I saw her a few times on the beach, playing with other girls her age. They were kids."

"I know. Did you ever see her with a guy?"

"No. The detective asked me that."

"Then I won't try to do his job. Is the coffee ready?"

"Yes, it is. Two coffees?"

"*Si, por favor,*" Daria said. She swept off her face a few stray hairs that in her hurry hadn't been captured in the pony tail. She looked sad.

"Does this kind of thing happen often?" Ronan asked.

"It happens too often. The girls don't often get killed, but they often get hurt. I don't understand why a guy would want to hurt a girl."

"I don't either."

"You're a guy. I was hoping you could enlighten me."

"I can't," he said. "I never felt like hurting a girl."

"You never were so angry at a girl that you wanted to hit her?"

He thought back. "No. I wanted to hurt their feelings, but I never wanted to hit them."

"Why did you want to hurt their feelings?"

"Because they hurt my feelings."

"So you wanted to get back at them?"

"Yeah. I wanted them to feel like I did."

"Okay. The girl could have hurt his feelings, and he could have wanted to get back at her. But what could she have said or done that would make him want to *kill* her?"

"Maybe she stirred up something deep inside of him."

"Like what?" Daria asked as if she simply couldn't fathom what it might have been.

"Maybe it was something he never forgave his mother for."

She looked at him attentively. "Is there something you never forgave your mother for?"

"Yeah, there is. My mother died when I was only five."

"I'm sorry," she said, reaching for his hand.

"It's all right. It happened twenty-eight years ago."

"And you still haven't forgiven her?"

"I know I should have, but I don't think I have. It's still lying there deep inside of me."

"But you wouldn't want to kill someone for stirring it up. You don't want to kill *me*, do you?"

"No," he said, smiling. After a long silence he asked: "Do you think the police will find the guy who did it?"

"I don't think so. By now he must have left the country. And no one at Arabian Nights will admit that she worked there."

"Not even the girls?"

Daria shook her head. "Their owner won't let them tell the police anything."

"Their owner? Are the girls who work there slaves?"

"Yeah. They're the property of that hotel, just as the slaves who used to work in the cane fields were the property of the plantations. It's the same relationship."

"Well, if no one will tell the police anything, then how will they identify the victim?"

"They might not ever be able to. If her mother sold her as a sex slave, she's certainly not going to come forward and identify her daughter."

"You mean mothers *sell* their children as sex slaves?"

"Where have you been?" Daria said. "The mother has a kid she can't support, she has no husband, she has a drug habit, and she needs money. Selling the kid is the quickest and easiest way to get money."

"That's revolting."

"It is, but what's more revolting is *buying* the kid's services. If there wasn't a market, the mother couldn't sell the kid."

At that moment Joop arrived with their coffees on a stainless steel server, along with sugar and cream and napkins.

"It's strong," Joop said, setting the server on the table.

"That's good. I need something to clear my head."

"If you need anything else, I'll be in the kitchen. My girl hasn't arrived yet."

"Thanks. If I need rum, I'll let you know."

Ronan waited for Daria to take one of the coffees, noticing that she didn't put anything into it, and then he took one for himself. He put some milk into his coffee and stirred it, asking: "Has anyone tried to shut down Arabian Nights?"

"My friend Filomena has been trying to shut them down since they opened almost two years ago. She's taken legal actions, and she's gotten the town council to pass resolutions asking the mayor to shut them down."

"You have a town council?"

"Oh, yes. But it has no power. It can only advise the mayor."

"Is the mayor elected?"

"Yes, he's elected."

"Then why," Ronan asked, "don't the people in this town vote the mayor out of office unless he shuts that place down?"

"The mayor doesn't have the power to shut it down."

"Doesn't he have the power of law?"

"Oh, yeah, he does," Daria said, "but that's not as strong as the power of money."

Ronan understood. He blew on the surface of his coffee and took a sip. "If I stay here for a while, I'll need something to do. I can't sit around and do nothing."

"Are you sure you want to stay here? As you're finding out, it's not a tropical paradise."

"I wasn't looking for a tropical paradise."

"What were you looking for?"

"I don't know. I guess I was looking for a getaway."

"There's something you want to get away from?"

"Yeah." He stopped abruptly, letting her know he wasn't ready to tell her what it was, and then he concluded: "So I can relate to the guys who sit at the round table."

"But they do nothing. You said you couldn't sit around and do nothing."

"I can't. I have to do something."

Daria paused to think and then asked: "Do you have any experience with accounting? I have to keep records for my donors, who want to know what I do with their money."

"I have some experience. While I was in graduate school I worked in the office of my father's company, helping with the accounts for his projects. So I know how to use accounting systems on a computer."

"Then you're hired. But I can't pay you anything."

"I don't need money. I need something to do."

"Okay. Then come to my clinic around four this afternoon."

When they had finished their coffee Daria left to go to work and Ronan walked down to the ocean, accompanied by the dog, evidently still hoping for a handout.

They avoided the spot where the body of the girl had lain.

Ronan stopped at the water's edge and took off his flip-flops. With one of them in each hand he started walking in the dry sand, which would give him more exercise than the sand that was packed almost solid by the waves.

There was no one else on the beach except for a team of four skinny black men with a donkey cart, raking the sand and picking up refuse left by the crowd on Sunday. As he approached them he heard them talking in a language that sounded like French, and he concluded that they were Haitians. They smiled amiably when he said: *"Bon jour."*

The beach, a perfect crescent, was about five miles long, and Joop's was in the middle of the curve, so if Ronan walked to the end and back it would burn some calories. At the end was a mountain, not as high as the one with Cristo on top of it, and that became his goal.

As he walked along the beach, with the trade wind at his back, his mind wandered back to the conversation with Daria and revolved around what he had told her about his mother. It had come from deep inside of him, where it had been festering for all those years, a wound in his soul that had never gone away. And maybe now was the time to examine it in the light, to expose it to the air where it could finally heal.

Presumably wanting to spare him and his older brother, his father had kept his mother's illness a secret from them. Of course in the days following her chemotherapy treatments they knew she wasn't feeling well, but they didn't know she had cancer, and they only found out when she had a few weeks left to live. By then it was clear even to a child that there was something terribly wrong with her. She lay in her bed and needed the help of a nurse to get up, and she had been reduced to skin and bones, though her sorrowful brown eyes were enormous.

She died in her sleep "peacefully" his father said, whatever that meant. For Ronan it meant that his mother had left them in the middle of the night and gone where they could never find her. It meant that she had chosen to do this. And he hated her for abandoning him, he hated God for being her accomplice, and he hated himself for hating her and for hating God.

When he saw the body in the casket he knew it wasn't her. They had made a wax figure that was supposed to look like her, though it really didn't. It looked like a wax figure, and it didn't fool him. It made him hate his father and the priest for going along with the fraudulent scheme. And though he sat through the funeral mass and went to the cemetery and watched them bury the casket, he refused to pray for her departed soul.

After the burial, while their house filled with relatives and friends, he went up to his room and closed the door and lay down on the bed with his face in the pillow and cried his heart out. Over and over he asked his mother: "Why did you leave me?"

39

At some point the door opened and his brother Gregory came into the room. His brother was nine, and with the age difference they didn't have much of a relationship.

"Are you all right?" Gregory asked.

"Go away," Ronan said with his voice muffled by the pillow.

"I know how you feel."

"No, you don't."

"She was *my* mother too."

"But you didn't love her like I did."

"How do you know?"

That stopped Ronan for a moment, but then he said: "I just know."

By then his brother was standing by the bed. "You don't know. I feel like you do."

He didn't argue, but he wasn't going to let Gregory share his grief, and when his brother sat down on the edge of the bed and put a hand on his shoulder, he said: "Don't touch me."

"We're brothers. We should stick together."

"I don't need you. Go away."

"We need each other."

"Go away."

After a long silence Gregory said: "All right. I'll go away."

He heard his brother close the door, and then he regretted his behavior. But he didn't get up and go after his brother.

A few hours later, when all the people had gone, the door opened again and his father came into the room.

"How are you doing, kid?" his father asked.

He didn't respond. He pressed his face deeper into the pillow.

"I know it's tough."

He still didn't respond. He had already had this conversation with his brother, and he didn't feel like repeating it.

"What happened to your mother was God's will, and we have to accept it."

"Maybe you do, but I don't have to."

"Yeah, you do. And think about your mother. She was in a lot of pain, and now it's over. Now she's with God."

"I don't want her to be with God, I want her to be with us."

"She's better off with God than with us."

"She wasn't happy with us?"

"She was, but then she got sick."

"Well, that's not my fault." Ronan said.

"It's not," his father agreed. "And it's not your fault that she died. But it's not her fault either. So don't blame her.'

"I don't blame her."

"It sounds like you do."

"I don't," he insisted, but he knew he did. He just didn't see any point in admitting it to his father, who had no idea how he felt.

"Your mother didn't want to get sick, and she didn't want to die. She didn't want to leave you without a mother. You have to understand that."

"Then why did she get sick and die?"

"I told you," his father said patiently. "It was God's will."

"Okay," he said, pretending to accept this explanation. He wished his father would go away and leave him alone in his sorrow.

And like his brother, his father finally did go away.

By the time he returned to Joop's they were open for business, and he spent the next hour or so there having breakfast. The dog was still with him, and though Ronan knew that if he gave the creature even the tiniest scrap of food he would probably never get rid of it, he set his plate of uneaten food down on the sand in front of it. As the dog ate, he felt its tail thumping on his foot. But when he left, the dog didn't follow him. Either the dog's minimal expectations had been met or it had spotted another prospect.

Back at his apartment, he roamed around for a while, not knowing what to do, and then he went out to the balcony with one of the books he had brought with him. He had been told it was a good place to catch up on your reading, so he had gone to the bookstore in Hastings and bought a dozen novels by authors he wanted to read.

41

Before sitting down he gazed out at the tranquil ocean, remembering that only this morning it had yielded up the body of that girl like a piece of food it couldn't stomach. And then he glanced over his shoulder toward the mountain, shrouded with clouds that completely hid Christ the Redeemer. He wondered if behind the dark clouds the girl was being welcomed by the outstretched arms, her sins forgiven.

After a few hours of reading he got restless, so he made a shopping list and walked into the center of town. He had *chicharrón de pollo* with rice and beans at Solo Chivo, and he bought a newspaper at Nelly's along with the items on his list. On an impulse he bought a packet of cigars called Principes. He wasn't a smoker, but his father enjoyed a good cigar and spoke highly of Dominican cigars. With his plastic bag of groceries he went to a bar across the street and ordered a shot of Brugal *sin hielo* and sat outside, smoking a cigar and sipping rum and reading the paper. This was the life, a voice told him.

When he had finished the cigar he walked back to his apartment and took a shower and changed his clothes and went out again, allowing himself a half hour to walk to the clinic and following the directions that Daria had given him. From the center of town he headed down the street opposite the church and immediately found himself in a different world. Here the buildings were one story, and while some were made of concrete blocks, most were made of wood panels painted light blue, light green, pink, yellow, or beige. And instead of terra cotta roofs, the buildings all had corrugated metal roofs.

The main street was gravel, not paved. Alongside was an open drainage ditch that had standing water in it. The side streets were mud, with ditches on the side and puddles in the middle. There were no cars, but now and then a motorbike raced down the street dodging holes and frightening chickens. And there were people on the street—old women, young men, and mothers with babies. At least half of the people he saw were mothers and babies. There were also children who had been at school, the boys in khaki pants and blue shirts and the girls in khaki skirts and blue blouses, their clothes still looking cleaned and pressed.

The street was lined with wooden poles from which electrical lines were strung, and most of the buildings had wires informally hooked up to the lines. From sounds of music and glimpses of moving pictures on screens inside the houses, Ronan gathered that electricity was used not only for lights but also for radio and television.

Down one street was a concrete building with "Baño" on its door, indicating a public bathroom, and he wondered where the sewage went. Presumably, it went into septic tanks, but since the *barrio* was at sea level, it must have found its way into the harbor. There were whiffs of raw sewage in the air flavoring the haze of smoke from the plant. His eyes were irritated, and he could feel noxious particles whizzing down his throat as he breathed. The worst bad air day in New York was nothing like this.

As instructed by Daria, he turned left at a *colmado* with a Presidente sign in front. The street gradually rose to about twenty feet above sea level, where there was less danger of flooding. And there on the right was the clinic, solidly built with concrete blocks that had been plastered over and painted white, with a corrugated metal roof that looked almost new. Like the other buildings in the *barrio* it was only one story, but it was a lot wider and deeper. Above the door was a sign in blue letters that said: "Clínica Altagracia."

Ronan entered and was greeted by a girl in a white smock seated at a reception desk.

"*Buenas tardes,*" the girl said with a smile. "How can I help you?"

"I'm here to see the doctor."

"You mean Dr. Sánchez?"

"I guess. Is her first name Daria?"

"*Sí, lo es.* She's with a patient right now, but if you give me your name I'll let her know you're here."

"I'm Ronan."

"Are you a patient?"

"No, I'm a friend."

Ronan sat down in one of the orange plastic chairs used by people waiting to see the doctor. On his right was a woman with a kid in her lap. The kid had a cough that sounded more serious than a cold. Was it chronic bronchitis?

The girl waited until a young woman with a baby in her arms came out of an office, and then she got up and went into the office.

A few minutes later Daria came out, and he rose to greet her.

"Thanks for coming," she said with a welcoming smile. "I'll show you where the papers are."

He followed her down a hall that had doors on each side with letters on them. At the end of the hall was a door without a letter, and she led him into it. The room had a table, two chairs, and a bookcase. On the table were piles of papers and a desktop computer.

"This is our office. It's the room we use the least. We're so busy with our patients, we don't have any time for papers."

"I guess you don't have to worry about health insurance."

She laughed. "No. That's one thing I don't miss about New York—filling out papers for insurance companies."

"How do your patients pay you?"

"They don't. Our services are free, thanks to our donors. The whole world should have a healthcare system like this, and maybe someday it will."

"Maybe. But I wouldn't hold my breath until that happens."

"I won't. Though, as you can see, we have other reasons to hold our breath."

"I smoked a cigar this afternoon. I didn't inhale. But walking through these streets, I felt like I was inhaling a cigar."

"It's worse than cigars."

"In the waiting room a kid was sitting next to me in his mother's lap. He had a cough that didn't sound good."

"It's not good. His name is Elvin, and he might live another year, *si Dios quiere*."

"I know why you have your clinic here. But why do you live here and breathe this air?"

She appraised him. "I think you know why."

"You want to breathe the same air as your patients?"

"That's right. As long as that plant pollutes their air, I'm going to breathe it."

He looked at her with open admiration. "Well, I don't want to keep you from your patients. Just show me where to start, and I can figure out what to do."

She explained what the different piles of papers were, and she showed him the forms they had to fill out with information for the donors. And then she left him.

Grateful to have something to do, he went to work. He started by looking to see what they had on the computer. They had some files, which hadn't been updated for several months, and when he compared the files with the forms, he found ways to improve the files so that they would be more useful. He spent the next two hours getting things organized. By the time Daria returned to the office Ronan felt like he had accomplished something.

"How are you doing?" she asked him.

"I'm doing fine." He explained to her what he had done.

"That's really helpful. One of my many deficiencies is a total lack of administrative skills."

"Whatever your skills, it's not what you should be doing anyway."

"Yeah, I keep telling myself that, but it always sounds like a rationalization."

"I think it's a valid justification."

"Speaking of justifications," she said, sitting down in the other chair, "I stopped by the church to pray for the soul of that poor girl, and I talked with Padre Tavarez. I told him I felt like blowing up the power plant, and I asked him if the just war doctrine would apply to that situation."

"What did he say?"

"He reviewed the conditions with me. The first is that the damage inflicted by the aggressor must be lasting, grave, and certain."

"The aggressor being the owner of the plant."

"That's right. And he agreed about the damage. The smoke is

killing people, and that's lasting, grave, and certain."

"I'm sure the owner would question the claim that the smoke is killing people."

"Yeah, like the tobacco companies questioned the claim that their products were killing people. But there's a mountain of evidence to support our claim."

"Okay," he said, going along with her.

"Next, we've tried all other means to stop the plant from polluting the air, and they've been impractical and ineffective."

"Did Padre Tavarez agree?"

"He did. He knows what we've done." She paused for a moment. "Next, there must be serious prospects of success. Well, if we blow up the plant, it'll stop the pollution."

"Until they bring in another plant."

"They won't bring in another plant. They're having problems, so they'll be glad to get out of this country. They'll take the insurance money and run."

"Okay. It'll stop the pollution."

"The last condition," Daria said, "is that the use of force must not produce evils or disorders graver than the evil to be eliminated. Well, if there's no one inside the plant when the bomb goes off, then no one will be hurt."

"They must always have someone inside the plant."

"They have a night shift of two workers. You only have to find a reason to get them both out of the plant before you set off the bomb."

"How would you do that?"

"We could create a diversion," Daria said. "For example, a fire in the tank farm."

"Okay. But even if you got them out of the plant, you'd still produce a disorder by blowing it up. You'd destroy an important source of power."

"Yeah, we'd have more outages for a while, but we've learned to live with them. And not having the power from that plant wouldn't be an evil or a disorder graver than killing people with its smoke."

"Did Padre Tavarez agree?"

"He did. He said the apostles lived without electricity."

"So blowing up the plant would meet the conditions of the doctrine?"

"It would. But Padre Tavarez had one question. He asked me how we could be absolutely sure that there was no one inside the plant when we blew it up."

"Did you have an answer to that question?"

"No. I didn't. And I still don't."

At that moment her cell phone rang. The ring tone was the opening bars of a hymn that he recognized but didn't know the name of, something about the power of God.

"*Hola?*" she said into the phone. "*Qué dices? Dios mio!*"

"What happened?" he asked after she had finished.

"Now we have a dead man."

"Where? On the beach?"

"No, he's hanging from the gate at Arabian Nights. I have to go there right away."

"Can I go with you?"

"You don't want to see what happened to him."

"I live here," Ronan told her. "I have a right to know what happened."

"Okay," Daria said with reservation. "Come on. Let's go."

There were no more patients waiting, so she asked the girl to lock up and she went out the front door, carrying a bag of instruments.

In front of the clinic was a motorbike, which she hopped on and started.

Without being told he got on behind her and looked for something to hold on to.

"Hold on to me," she said, revving the engine.

He put his arms around her waist. Though she had curves, her body was firm—it didn't have the slightest layer of fat.

As they sped off he had to move closer and tighten his grip to avoid sliding back, so his hands were now around her abdomen. In this position, they had an urge to move up and feel her breasts, which of course he suppressed.

She drove carefully, having seen the results of motorbikes hitting holes and flinging their riders into ditches or trees or walls of buildings. And she took the corners slowly, aware of the sand in which they could easily slide out of control.

Within ten minutes they pulled up in front of Arabian Nights, where there was a group of people standing in front of the gate.

Daria parked her motorbike behind the police van and headed toward them.

When he saw what had happened Ronan understood why Daria had tried to dissuade him from coming with her.

Hanging from the gate in a noose was the naked body of a large blond man. His penis had been cut off and stuffed into his mouth with the tip pointing out. And tied to his chest was a sign that said: "This is what happens to foreigners who exploit our children."

Ronan stopped and stared, appalled, while Daria joined the guy in plainclothes who had been on the beach that morning. He overheard her say: "I think the cause of death is obvious."

"You mean he didn't die from the operation," the guy in plainclothes muttered.

"He died from asphyxiation. I can see that from here."

"So we can cut him down?"

"If it was my decision," she said bluntly, "I'd leave him there. I'd let him rot there. It would have the desired effect on their clients."

"I can't do that."

"I know you can't."

As a uniformed cop emerged from the courtyard with a ladder Ronan noticed an image in the lower right corner of the sign. It was a cobra with its head raised, ready to strike.

"They didn't take long," the guy in plainclothes said.

"They understand the principles of behavioral psychology," Daria said. "To be effective, a reward or a punishment should immediately follow the behavior."

"There were six of them. They arrived in jeeps at five thirty-five. They had automatic weapons, and they took over. They made everyone stand against a wall while two of them went from room to room to find a victim. They found this guy with a girl about the same age as the girl on the beach. He's a gross German, so he was perfect."

"I wonder if his wife knew he was here."

"If he didn't care about his wife, why should we?"

"That's a good question."

Daria stayed long enough to examine the body and verify her opinion on the cause of death, and then she rejoined Ronan, asking: "Do you still want to stay here?"

"Yeah. I do." He couldn't explain why, so he didn't attempt to.

"Okay. You know, I don't agree with the method of the guys who did this, but maybe it'll shut the place down."

"It'll scare away clients."

"That would make Filomena happy. We were planning to get together this evening to talk about that girl, but now we have even more to talk about."

"Can I join you?" Ronan asked.

"Before we go any further," Daria said, folding her arms, "I need to know what your motives are. I mean, are you just looking for something to do?"

"I *am* looking for something to do. But I'm also looking for a mission."

"What about teaching? Isn't that your mission?"

"It is, but I'm on a leave of absence."

"So you're looking for an interim mission?"

"It could be longer than interim."

"You know my mission. It's to make that plant stop killing people. Do you think you could commit yourself to that?"

"I think I could. I've seen what you do."

"You haven't seen much of what I do. You've only seen me examine bodies."

"I've seen enough to understand what you're doing."

"Then you can join us," Daria said. "We're meeting at the pizza place in town. It's called Roma. It's on the main street near the central plaza. We'll be there at eight."

"I'll see you then."

He watched her mount the bike and start it and wheel it around. He admired her command of the bike as she jetted away, leaving a trail of dust behind her. All the elements were there for Ronan to fall in love with her.

FOUR

ROMA WAS AN open space under a roof of palm fronds that was filled with people when he arrived. The smoke in the air came not from the power plant but from the wood fire of the pizza oven, where two young men in black shirts were busy making pies.

A woman with a regal aspect in a purple dress and spike heels swept toward him, saying: "Welcome to Roma. Are you meeting someone?"

Though the woman was speaking in Italian, Ronan was able to understand her. "Yes. I see them."

Daria was sitting at a corner table with a blond woman who at that moment was gesticulating.

Following his eyes, the hostess said: "You're in good company. *Buon appetito!*"

When he reached the table both women got up.

"Filomena, this is Ronan."

"*Mucho gusto,*" he said, shaking her hand.

"*Un gran placer,*" Filomena said in a clear high voice. Her blue eyes looked happy and her blond hair looked natural. Her skin was lighter than Daria's but not white. She wore a loose long-sleeved white shirt with the cuffs turned back, and around her neck was a simple cord from which hung a wooden cross. "You can call me Filo."

The word in Spanish meant the edge of a knife, which didn't seem to go with her appearance.

They all sat down.

Daria asked: "What kind of pizza would you like?"

"Oh, any kind," he said truthfully.

"We like the *margherita* with fresh garlic."

"That sounds good."

"What would you like to drink?"

"I'll have white wine," he said, noticing a half-full carafe of it on the table.

Daria signaled to the waitress, who came right over, and she ordered a large *margherita* pie with fresh garlic.

"We were talking about what happened today at Arabian Nights," Daria said when the waitress had left them.

"You seem to know who did it," he said.

"We know it was the Cobras. They left their logo on the sign."

"I noticed that. Who are the Cobras?"

"They're a band of guerrillas who actually do what we feel like doing," Filo said.

"You feel like killing sex tourists?"

"Every single one of them," Filo said. "I fantasize about killing them. I even imagine doing things like what they did to that German. But I never would."

"Why wouldn't you?"

"I believe that life is sacred. I believe that nothing justifies taking the life of a human being."

"We both believe that," Daria said.

"Well, what if you were cornered," Ronan asked them, "by a guy who was going to kill you? Would you defend yourselves?"

"Of course we would," Filo said. "But we wouldn't have to kill him."

"What would you do?"

"We'd kick him in the *cojones*," Daria said.

"To be honest," Filo said, "I don't condone what they did to that German, but for almost two years I've been trying to have the place shut down, and I've gotten nowhere. What the Cobras did might finally put it out of business."

"You don't condone what they did," Ronan said, "but you'd be happy if they got results."

"I would be," Filo admitted.

Ronan paused. "So what do you know about them?"

"We don't know much about them," Daria said. "We just

know they're guys who believe that violence is the only way to solve problems."

"Would you call them terrorists?"

"I wouldn't," Filo said. "They use violence to achieve a political goal, but they don't kill innocent people."

"They killed a man who was innocent of killing that girl."

"But he exploited girls like her, so he wasn't innocent."

"You mean there was some justice in what they did to him."

"Yeah, there was," Filo said. "In their own way they did what the government fails to do."

"She's talking about how the government fails to enforce the law against having sex with underage children," Daria said.

"Then would you call them vigilantes?"

"That's more accurate than calling them terrorists."

"Okay," Ronan said. "Besides killing that German, what other things like that have they done?"

"The last thing was the drug dealer," Filo said.

"That happened about two months ago," Daria said.

"A fourteen-year-old boy died of an overdose. So two days later they killed the dealer. They left his body in front of the house of a drug lord in Santo Domingo."

"They gave him an overdose of his own drugs."

"They put a sign on him that said 'This is what happens to drug dealers who kill our children.' "

"Before that, a ten-year-old boy died from being run over by a car. So a few days later they killed the driver, who was a rich man. They ran him over repeatedly with his Mercedes. They left a sign on him that said: 'This is what happens to reckless drivers who kill our children.' "

"There's a common theme," Ronan said.

"Yeah, it's always about children," Daria said.

"I have a question. Do you think they know what the power plant is doing to children?"

"They must know. Everyone knows."

"Then if you want to blow up the plant, they might help you."

Daria shook her head, saying: "I wouldn't get involved with

them. If they blew up the plant, they wouldn't care if there were people inside it."

"They don't mind killing people," Filo said.

"But if you made sure that there was no one inside the plant when they blew it up, then maybe you could work together. I mean, you have the same goals."

"We have the same goals," Daria said, "but we have different methods of achieving them."

"Though at times we do wonder," Filo said, "if their method is more effective."

At that moment the pizza arrived, smelling of garlic.

As they started eating, Filo said: "Daria told me you're helping with her paperwork. Could you help with mine?"

"Yeah, sure. Where are you located?"

"On the other side of town. Daria agreed to share you with me, so if you're free tomorrow morning, I'll show you what to do."

"Okay. Well, it looks like I won't be idle here."

"We'll see to that," Daria said, chewing on a bite of pizza.

Before they left the restaurant Filo told him how to get to her center, and then they went their separate ways: Daria toward the *barrio*, Filo toward the other side of town, and Ronan toward the ridge. As he walked along the main street he could hear the power plant rumbling in the distance, and he stopped to look back at the night sky. There was a full moon, and in its light he could see the smoke rising toward the mountain, toward the arms of Christ. It was as if the plant was defying Him to stop it from polluting the air.

He continued walking with the image of Filomena in his mind. The blue eyes and the blond hair had reminded him of someone, and now he realized who it was.

Within two years of his mother's death his father brought a woman home for them to meet. He introduced her as his secretary. Her name was Molly, and even at the age of seven Ronan could tell she was a lot younger than his father.

There had been au pair girls to take care of them, girls from Europe with strange accents, as well as the woman who cooked for them and cleaned the house, but Molly didn't act like an au pair girl, she acted like a girlfriend.

Outraged that his father would bring home a girlfriend, Ronan refused to meet her, and he ran upstairs to his room and closed the door. His father pursued him and tried to coax him into going back down to the living room, but Ronan wouldn't budge. In protest he remained in his room for the rest of the evening, going without dinner.

Later, his father came back to his room and talked with him.

"You weren't very nice to Molly," his father told him.

"Why should I be nice to her?"

"Because I like her."

"I don't like her."

"How do you know you don't like her?"

"I just know."

"Well, next time I want you to be nice to her."

"Is she coming here again?"

"Yes. She is. Eventually she may come here to stay."

"Are you going to marry her?"

"I'm thinking about it."

"I don't want you to marry her."

"If you get to know her, I think you'll like her. She's a warm, loving person. And we need someone like her in this house."

"I don't need her."

"I think you do. And I know I need her."

"What does Greg think about her?"

"He likes her."

"Then you and Greg can have her, but I don't want her."

His father sighed. "The au pair girls are nice, but you need something more than that. You need a mother."

"I have a mother."

"She's with God now."

"She's still with me."

"I know, but it's not the same as actually being here. She can't take care of you from heaven."

"Yes, she can."

His father reached out and took his hand. "Well, all I'm asking is for you to give Molly a chance. Will you do that for me?"

"All right," he finally said, but his mind was already closed on the subject.

Over the next few months his father brought Molly home for dinner on Fridays. His father also brought pizza, which they ate together in the kitchen like a family. Ronan didn't participate much in the conversation, but when Molly addressed him he responded politely.

After one such evening his father asked: "Are you getting to know her?"

"Yeah," he said. "And I still don't like her."

"What don't you like about her?"

"I don't know." In fact, the only thing he didn't like about her was her evident intention of marrying his father. If she had been another au pair girl, he would have liked her fine.

"Well, she likes you."

"How could she like me? She doesn't know me."

"She knows you well enough. And if she didn't like you," his father said to prove the point, "she wouldn't want to marry me."

"Do you want to marry her?"

"Yes. So I'd like your permission."

"What if I don't give it to you?"

"Then I won't marry her."

He believed his father, and for a moment he liked having this kind of power over his father, but then he realized that it was only the power to make his father unhappy. So he finally said: "You have my permission to marry her."

"I love you, Ronan," his father said, leaning toward him.

Ronan said nothing, backing away from the kiss that was aimed at his forehead.

From then until the wedding Molly not only had dinner with them on Fridays but also spent Saturdays with them and joined them on Sundays for noon mass at St. Joseph's in Bronxville. His father had introduced her to the priest, who greeted her warmly as they filed out of church after the mass. It was clear that the priest had given his blessing to the marriage.

One Sunday afternoon while his father and Gregory were watching a football game on television, Molly opened the door of his room and asked: "Can I come in?"

"Sure," he said. He was lying on his bed with a coloring book.

She sat down on the edge of the bed.

He made room for her.

"I like what you've done," she said, referring to the scene of a farm that he was coloring. "Now, what about the cows?"

He hadn't decided about the cows.

"Are they dairy cows?"

"I don't know."

"They can be whatever you want them to be."

"I guess I want them to be dairy cows."

"Then they should be either black and white or light brown."

He thought about it, and then he reached for the brown crayon and started coloring one of the cows. He could smell her perfume, which he didn't dislike, but it wasn't how he remembered the smell of his mother.

"That's a Brown Swiss," she told him.

"How do you know?"

"I'm from upstate New York. It's dairy country. We had cows everywhere."

"Why didn't you stay there?"

"There were no jobs, no opportunities. So I went away to college."

"Where did you go?"

"St. Catherine."

He remembered driving by a place with that name. It was over near the river. But he hadn't known it was a college.

"I know I can never replace your mother," she said after a silence, "but I want to be the next best thing. Will you give me a chance?"

He didn't respond. He just kept coloring the cow.

"I already know you well enough to love you, Ronan, and the more I get to know you, the more I'll love you."

He couldn't imagine her loving him. In fact, he couldn't

imagine anyone loving him. If he had been worthy of love, then his mother wouldn't have left him.

"Will you give me a chance?" she asked him again.

"Okay," he said, but only to get rid of her.

"Thank you," she said, and she leaned over and softly kissed the back of his neck.

When she had gone, he wiped off the spot where she had kissed him.

The wedding was in May at St. Joseph's. He and his brother were in the wedding party, dressed identically in blue blazers, gray pants, white shirts, and bright red ties. He watched in dismay as his father promised to be true to Molly in good times and in bad, in sickness and in health, and to love her and honor her all the days of his life.

The reception was at his father's country club, and while they were giving toasts he wandered out and started walking across the golf course. He had no destination, he only wanted to get as far away as possible, but the ends of the earth weren't far enough.

Standing on the green of the eighth hole he realized that at some point they would notice he was missing, and they would be upset. As much as he objected to the wedding, he didn't want to spoil it for his father, so he headed back.

They were still doing toasts, and they hadn't missed him.

The next morning he did his walk on the beach, accompanied by the stray dog, which had met him on the road as if it knew his schedule.

When he returned to Joop's he decided to have breakfast there at the round table, where a few guys had already gathered. Donal was among them, and he introduced Ronan to them.

"We were talking about what the Cobras did to that German at Arabian Nights," Donal said.

"You should have seen him hanging on the gate," Willem said as if he would never forget the sight.

"I'm glad I didn't," Hans said.

"It was awful," Willem said.

"I heard they caught him with a twelve-year-old girl," Donal said. "If that's true, then he deserved what they did to him."

"You really think so?" Hans said.

"Yeah, I do. Having sex with kids is disgusting."

"Your priests had sex with kids."

"I know they did. And that was disgusting. They deserved what happened to that German."

"But they got off light. So there's no justice."

"Yes, there is. What happened to that German was justice."

"It's going to hurt Arabian Nights," Willem said.

"I hope it puts them out of business," Donal said. "Imagine using kids as prostitutes."

"But that's the attraction," Hans said. "You can find legal-age prostitutes anywhere."

"I think the Cobras are fascinating," Willem said.

"You wouldn't," Hans said, "if they cut off your *schwanz* and stuffed it into your mouth."

"They wouldn't ever have a reason to do that," Willem said. "I wouldn't ever go to that place."

"I wouldn't either," Hans said. "I've done enough bad shit to last a lifetime. Joop, can you bring me another?"

"I wonder who they are," Willem said.

"You mean the Cobras?" Hans said.

"Well, I didn't mean the Dutch football team."

"I think they're guys like us," Ronan said.

"The Dutch football team?"

"No. The Cobras."

"They're not guys like us," Willem said. "I can't imagine doing the things they do."

"I can," Ronan admitted. "I'd never do them, but I can imagine doing them."

"There must be something wrong with you," Willem said.

"There's nothing wrong with him," Hans said. "He's just being honest. We can all imagine doing things like the Cobras do. And we're all capable of doing them."

"Speak for yourself," Willem said.

"I'm speaking for all of us."

"You don't have a right to speak for all of us."

"Yeah, I do," Hans said testily.

"We've all done things," Donal said, "that other people think are bad. If we hadn't, we wouldn't be here."

"Maybe we have," Willem said. "But we don't do things like the Cobras do."

"Well, if we were in their situation," Hans said, "we might do things like they do."

"We might," Ronan said. "But we might not. I mean, we know people in their situation who don't do things like they do."

"Who are you talking about?"

"He's talking about Daria and Filo," Donal said.

"How are they in the same situation as the Cobras?"

"They have the same goal as the Cobras," Ronan said. "They want social justice."

"I wasn't talking about what saints might do," Hans said. "I was talking about what *we* might do in their situation."

"But we're not Cobras," Willem said.

"And we're not saints," Hans said.

That left them in the middle, capable of going either way.

"I see you've made friends with Daria," Donal said to Ronan.

"She's an attractive woman," Hans said.

"Has she ever had a boyfriend?" Willem asked.

"Not that I know of," Hans said.

"She's a vestal virgin," Donal said. "At least that's what her namesake was."

"Who was her namesake?" Willem asked.

"St. Daria, an early Christian martyr."

"Who were the vestal virgins?"

"They were women who took a vow of chastity and served as priests of Vesta, the goddess of the hearth. Their main duty was to maintain a sacred fire, where people could come and get fire for their homes."

"What if they had sex?"

"They were punished by being buried alive."

"That would be an effective deterrent."

"They had a lot of privileges, which also deterred them from having sex."

"You mean from getting caught."

"What happened to St. Daria?" Willem asked.

"She was forced to marry the son of a great nobleman, whose name was Chrysanthus. He had become a Christian, and he converted Daria. They lived together like brother and sister, but the emperor didn't like Christians, so he arrested them and tortured them. He finally buried them alive in a deep pit and covered them with stones."

"Do you think our Daria is a virgin?" Willem asked.

"She's not maintaining a sacred fire," Hans said.

"No. She's not," Donal agreed. "If anything, she's trying to put out a fire."

"You mean the power plant," Ronan said.

"Did she show you what it does?"

"Yes. She showed me."

"She showed all of us. But if she wants action, she should show the Cobras what that plant does."

"You think they don't know what it does?"

"No, I don't think they know," Donal said. "If they did, they'd do something about it."

"What would they do?" Ronan asked.

"They'd drop the manager down the chimney," Willem said.

"They'd steam the engineer to death," Hans said.

"So Ronan was right," Donal said, laughing. "The Cobras *are* guys like us."

"They're not," Willem insisted. "We're only imagining what they would do. We're not actually doing those things."

"But we're capable of doing them," Hans said.

The dog, which had been lying at Ronan's feet, perked up at the smell of the food that Joop was bringing to the table.

After breakfast Ronan returned to his apartment. While standing in the shower he happened to look out the window and see the statue of Christ on top of the mountain. Unnerved by the sight, he looked away from the window. He soaped himself and rinsed himself, and when he looked out the window again the statue was hidden behind a cloud.

When he left his building he headed toward the other side of town. Beyond the ridge there were fewer houses and more open land, including pastures where horses were grazing.

At one point Ronan paused to watch some kids at the base of an enormous tree, throwing sticks up into the branches. When something plopped to the ground, he realized that they were trying to knock fruit out of the tree.

"You want a mango?" a kid asked him. "Only two dollars."

"I don't have dollars. How many pesos?"

The kid didn't seem to know, so Ronan exchanged a hundred pesos for the mango, which was perfectly ripe. It was smaller than the mangos they sold back home, more shaped like a kidney, and it smelled like wine.

Following the directions Filo had given him, Ronan arrived at a two-story building that could have once been a small hotel.

He rang the bell, and within a minute the door opened.

"*Hola*," Filo said with a warm smile. She was wearing white shorts and a white polo shirt, which accentuated her tan color. She had long legs and long arms. "Come on in."

"I brought you a present," he said, offering her the mango.

She accepted it, saying: "Thank you. I love mangos."

He went into a hall, which had no furniture but had several unopened boxes lying on the floor and a bicycle leaning against the wall.

"Would you like coffee?"

"No, thanks. I had enough at Joop's."

"His coffee is strong."

He followed her into the next room, which had benches on both sides of an aisle and a table in front with a chair behind it. On the wall above the table was a crucifix.

"This is our assembly room," she told him. "We say prayers every morning, and we have communion on Wednesday evenings."

"With Daria serving as extraordinary minister?"

"Yeah, how did you guess?"

"I received the host from her on Sunday."

"Daria is a saint. I can't imagine what I'd do without her."

"According to her, you're a saint."

"No, I'm a sinner," Filo said in a low voice as if she didn't want people to hear. And then she brightened. "Well, let me explain our mission to you. We have two objectives—to prevent our children from being exploited for commercial sex, and to rescue those who have become victims."

"Is that a major problem in this country?"

"Unfortunately, it is. More than fifty thousand underage children are exploited for commercial sex in this country."

"What's the legal age of consent?"

"It's eighteen."

"That's higher than it is in most of our states."

"I know, but it doesn't mean anything. Like so many of the laws here, it's not enforced."

"It's not enforced in our country. They arrest the girls, not the guys who have broken the law."

Without commenting on that injustice Filo continued: "In our prevention program we target children who drop out of school or are problem children or have a history of suspected abuse. We work with the schools to identify them, and then we give them remedial education to improve their academic skills and their social behavior. Before or after their shift in a regular school they have a shift in our school. In the summer they spend the whole day in our school."

"How old are they?"

"They're between the ages of nine and fifteen. When they reach fifteen we start teaching them skills for the workplace."

"What kinds of skills?"

"Computer skills and other trade skills. We used to teach sewing, which helped them get jobs in the Zona Franca, but the clothing factories moved to China, so we now put more emphasis on skills that will help them get jobs in tourism."

"Where do these children live?" Ronan asked.

"They live at home, and they go to school. That's one of our conditions—they have to go to school."

"I heard that the schools in Puerto Plata have three shifts."

"The public schools do. We have a Catholic school in Santa Cruz where they can go all day."

"Is that the school Katiuska goes to?"

"Yes. She's in our rescue program. She was a sex slave, along with nineteen other girls and boys. They don't have families, or they don't have families that they should be living with, so they live here. We have five rooms upstairs, with four to a room. We have sixteen girls and four boys."

"Were they all sold into slavery?"

"Some of them were, and others were lured into it by the promise of material things."

"Were many of them at Arabian Nights?"

"Only a few of them," Filo said. "Most of them worked in Puerto Plata and other cities."

"Do they receive the same services as the other children?"

"Yes. They all get help with their academic skills, they all get training for the workplace, and they all get education in health, human rights, and human dignity."

"Where do you get funding for your programs?"

"Wherever we can," Filo said. "We get most of it from private foundations. We don't get any support from the government."

"Do you get money from foreign sources?"

"We get most of it from foreign sources. There's not a lot of money in this country. But there are Dominicans in your country who have a lot of money. You know, there are more than a hundred Dominican baseball players who make at least a million dollars a year."

"I read about them in *Hoy* every day."

"So I'm working on them, and one of them already gave me a hundred thousand dollars."

"That's great," Ronan said. "They should be a good source."

"Well, let me show you a classroom," Filo said, heading for a door.

They went into a room where four children were seated around a table with a young woman.

"Hi, Inés. Please don't mind us. I'm just showing this gentleman around."

The young woman smiled at him and then returned to her work. She was wearing a tee shirt that said: *"Son nuestros muchachos y hay que defenderlos."*

After they had left the room Filo explained: "She's helping those children learn to read."

"They looked about nine."

"They are, but they don't know how to read yet."

"Have they been going to school?"

"Yes, but they haven't been learning. You must have that problem in your country."

"We do," he admitted. "We have high school graduates who can't read."

"Well, if they can't read, they can't learn anything, and they're at risk for exploitation—all types of exploitation."

"I understand," he said, based on his own experience.

She led him through some other rooms where classes were being held, and finally she led him into a kitchen, where a girl and a boy were preparing a meal.

"They take turns in the kitchen," Filo explained. "Some of them like cooking, and some of them don't. You guys like cooking, right?"

"Right," the girl said. "We're making *habichuelas.*"

"They smell good," Ronan said.

After the kitchen they came to a staircase, which Filo led him up with a spring in her step.

"Was this building a hotel?" he asked her.

"No. It was a school, a private school. It went out of business three years ago."

"There weren't enough children in the town to support it?"

"There were, but the school wasn't making money."

"You mean it was for profit?"

"Yes. They charged a high tuition, but since they wouldn't pay enough to get good teachers it wasn't worth what the parents were paying."

"So you found a better use for the building."

"In this country you have to be *muy aprovechado*."

She led him down a hall that had open doors on each side. From what he could see, the beds were made and the rooms were neat.

"How long do they live here?"

"Until they can support themselves. We hope they leave by the time they're twenty-one, and they usually do."

"As they get older do they ever have—relationships with each other?"

"You mean sex? They really don't have much interest in sex after what they've been through. They need to have a loving relationship before they can appreciate sex."

He had the feeling that Filo was speaking from experience.

They were downstairs in a back office, and she was showing him how he could help with her paperwork when a young woman in one of those tee shirts interrupted.

"There's a policeman at the front door," the woman said nervously. "He wants to see you."

"Please show him the way to this office. I'll see him here."

"Do you want me to leave?" Ronan asked.

"I want you to stay. I mean, if you will."

"I will. I'm here to help you."

"*Gracias.* In these situations it never hurts to have a guy on your side."

A few minutes later the guy in plainclothes who had been at the beach and at the gate of Arabian Nights appeared in the doorway. His face was impassive with more than a hint of weariness in his blood-shot eyes.

"I'm sorry to bother you," he said politely.

"*No hay problema,*" Filo told him. "How can I help you?"

"I have to ask you some questions about what happened at Arabian Nights."

"Okay. Please sit down. Would you like coffee?"

"No, thanks." The guy sat down and reached into his pocket for a card, which he handed to Filo. He glanced at Ronan suspiciously.

"He's my advisor," Filo said. "He's from New York. His name is Ronan Byrne."

"Sergio Herrera," the detective said, extending his hand.

"*Mucho gusto,*" Ronan said.

"*Igualmente,*" Sergio said.

"*Estoy a su disposición,*" Filo said.

Sergio cleared his throat and said: "According to our records, you've been very active in trying to have Arabian Nights shut down. You've presented resolutions to the town council, you've initiated legal actions, and you've organized pickets against their business."

"With good reason. It violates our laws on zoning, sexual consent, and child labor, not to mention the commandments of our religion."

"They have a permit."

"And you know how they got it."

"They got it through the normal process."

"They did. They paid for it. But however they got it," Filo continued, "it doesn't give them the right to exploit children, to enslave them, and to kill them."

"We have no evidence that they killed that girl."

"You know it was one of their clients."

"We don't know that. We have no idea who killed her."

"Then you're not conducting a serious investigation."

"We are," Sergio insisted. "That's why I'm here."

"Well, I can't help you find the guys who killed that German."

"We thought you could."

"Why did you think that?"

"You and those guys have the same goal."

"We do," Filo said. "But we don't use the same method."

"Maybe you don't, but I don't hear you condemning what they did."

"I condemn it. Killing that German was a mortal sin."

"All right. You condemn what they did. But how do I know it wasn't your idea?"

"You don't know. But even if it *had* been my idea—which of course it wasn't—I didn't have a way of giving it to the Cobras."

"I think you did. I think you're in contact with them."

"I don't know who they are or where they are."

"I think you do know."

"Well, you can think whatever you want," Filo said. "But I'm not in contact with the Cobras, I have never been in contact with them, and I will never be in contact with them. I'm against using violence."

"We're all against using violence," Sergio said, "until we find that nothing else works."

"I haven't reached that point. I still believe in our approach."

"Your approach doesn't seem to be working."

"It *is* working. I just took this gentleman on a tour, and he saw what we're doing for these children. Come with me and see for yourself."

"I don't have time," Sergio said, rising from his chair.

"But you have time to question me."

"I have to pursue all leads."

"Then you should go to Arabian Nights and find out who that girl's last client was."

"They say she never worked there. Even the girls say she never worked there."

"One of your cops said she worked there."

"He did, but he later decided that he was mistaken."

Filo nodded. "You mean he was paid to change his story."

"That doesn't happen. And I'm putting you on notice," Sergio said. "If we ever find out that you've had any contact with the Cobras, we're going to arrest you, and we're going to charge you with being an accessory. *Entiendes?*"

"*Entiendo.* Have a good day."

When the detective had left them Ronan said: "I assume you didn't want me to get involved in that conversation."

"You assumed correctly. I wanted you as a witness, and you were perfect in that role."

"From what he said, I gather that the police are more interested in pursuing the case of the German than the case of the girl."

"The girl was no one. The German was a tourist, and word will get back to Germany that it's not safe to come here. And that will hurt tourism."

"Unlike sex slavery, which helps tourism."

"You got it." For a while Filo was silent, and then she said: "I wasn't entirely truthful with the detective. I mean, part of me condemns what the Cobras did, but another part of me applauds it."

"That's understandable."

"Maybe it is, but I shouldn't applaud what they did to that poor guy."

"Don't waste your pity on him," Ronan told her.

"Okay. I won't," Filo murmured. "I need all the pity I have for the victims of people like him."

FIVE

BY THE END of the week Ronan had a daily routine that began with a walk on the beach, followed by breakfast at the round table, a shower, and a walk to Filo's center, where he worked for a few hours. Then he went back to his apartment and had a sandwich on the balcony, where he stayed for the next few hours reading. Then he walked to Daria's clinic, where he stayed until she closed for the day. Of course, she never really closed since she lived next to the clinic, and all the people in the *barrio* knew that if they had an emergency they could knock on her door.

About twice a week he had dinner with Daria and Filo at Roma or at Solo Chivo. The two women shared their frustrations over the lack of support from the government, and Ronan listened, wishing he could do more for them. He had no training in medicine, but he did have experience at teaching, so he thought about offering to help Filo in the classrooms. But he decided to hold back until her office was under control.

By now he knew the names of the guys who were regulars at the round table. Some of them came for breakfast and sat there all day. Others dropped by for a coffee or a beer or a plate of chicken, rice, and beans. They were permanent residents, and sometimes they talked about their work, but usually they talked about other things. They were mostly from Canada, Germany, England, and the Netherlands, and they spoke English as a common language, though in pairs they would revert to their native languages. They never spoke Spanish with each other, but they spoke it with the girls who worked at the restaurant and with the girls who joined them at the table while the sun was setting over the ridge.

Ronan was sitting among them at the round table having

breakfast on Friday morning when Willem pulled up in his car and joined them.

"Guess what they've done," Willem said, sitting down.

"You can't be talking about the government," Donal said, "because they never do anything."

"He must be talking about the Dutch football team," Hans said after sipping his coffee.

"I'm talking about the Cobras," Willem said.

"Did they string up another German?" Donal asked.

"No. They posted a picture of him on the website of Arabian Nights."

"I assume it's not a picture of him at his wedding."

"It's a picture of him hanging from the gate with his *lul* stuffed into his mouth."

"What a great idea," Hans said. "But how did the Cobras post a picture on that website?"

"One of them must have hacking skills," Willem said.

"Or else they hired a hacker to do it."

"*Ja,* you can hire a hacker to do anything."

"Maybe a competitor did it," Donal suggested.

"I don't think so," Willem said. "It would scare people from going to any of those places."

"It would scare me," Hans said. "Not that I need scaring. The risk of getting AIDS is enough to stop me from going to any of those places."

"It must be hurting their business," Ronan said.

"I'm sure it is," Donal said. "But if you want to know, you should go and see."

"You should check the place out," Hans agreed. "We've all done that. We went there for breakfast."

"What was it like?"

"It was like a normal hotel," Hans said. "You wouldn't guess what they do there."

"Until they offer you a girl," Willem said.

"Or a boy," Donal said.

Ronan had qualms about going there, but he decided that it

71

would be useful to know what was happening there, and he would have something to tell Filo. So instead of going directly back to his apartment, he headed for the street that was lined with palms.

As soon as Ronan turned the corner he saw that there were no cars parked along the street in front of the place as there usually were, on both sides.

Stopping at the gate, he looked in and saw no activity.

He entered the place and after stopping to look around he headed across the courtyard to the restaurant. There was no one at the tables.

To see what would happen, he sat at a table. Beyond the restaurant he saw a swimming pool around which girls in bikinis were lying in the sun.

A pretty girl in shorts and a top that exposed her cleavage as well as her navel appeared out of nowhere, asking: "Can I help you, sir?"

"If you're open, I'd like a coffee."

"We're open. How would you like it?"

"With milk," he said.

The girl turned and went to fetch it.

He was captivated by the sway of her ass in the tight shorts.

Before she returned, a woman in her mid-forties appeared. She had beady eyes and a parrot nose. She appraised him, saying: "Welcome to Arabian Nights. Is this your first time here?"

"Yes," he said. "I thought I might get a coffee here."

The woman smiled as if she understood his reluctance to admit his real reason for coming there. "Our coffee is good."

"That's what I heard."

"What else did you hear about us?"

Ronan shrugged. "Nothing."

"Well, I'll show you what we have to offer." She turned toward the pool and yelled: "Lucy! Elvira! Come here."

Obediently, two girls got up from their towels and headed for the restaurant.

Meanwhile the girl in shorts brought his coffee and set it

down on the table in front of him and then withdrew as if her job was done.

As they approached, Ronan could see how young the girls were—they couldn't have been more than fourteen. And their bikinis revealed almost everything.

They came to the table and presented themselves with shyly lowered eyes.

"What do you think?" the woman asked him.

"They're pretty," he said, swallowing.

"Girls, turn around."

The girls turned, displaying their asses. The bottoms of their bikinis covered only about half of their cracks.

He could feel those beady eyes watching him.

"Now, turn again and give him a peek."

The girls turned and enticingly lowered the tops of their bikinis, giving him a peek at their budding breasts.

"I'll tell you what," the woman said. "Since business is slow, I'll give you two for the price of one. They'll do anything you want. So what do you say?"

Ronan said nothing, ashamed of what he imagined doing.

The girls finally raised their eyes, and he saw how young and vulnerable they were. He felt they were asking him to let them go back to the swimming pool and play in the water like normal kids instead of using them to satisfy his bestial lust.

"I'm not interested," he lied, getting up.

"I can see that you are," the woman said, gazing at his pants.

"You can't see anything. You can't see what you're doing to these kids."

"They're not kids. They're eighteen. Aren't you, girls."

The girls nodded obediently.

He wanted to take them each by the hand and lead them out of there, but he was sure that the woman had goons to stop him and hold him until the police arrived to charge him with attempted robbery. So he left them for now, intending to rescue them later.

73

Even after taking a shower he still felt dirty, and when he arrived at Filo's center he still felt guilty for being aroused by those underage girls.

"What's the matter?" Filo asked as she let him in.

"Oh, nothing," he said, not wanting to admit to her of all people what the woman with the beady eyes had exposed in him.

"Something's the matter. Tell me."

He hesitated. "All right. But wait until we're in the office."

They went to the office and closed the door and remained standing.

"You look like you did something awful," Filo said after searching his face.

"I did. I mean, I feel like I did."

"Then tell me about it. I won't judge you."

He took a long breath, looking for a place to begin. "This morning I had breakfast at Joop's, and I heard that someone posted a picture of that German on the website of Arabian Nights. Did you hear that?"

"No. I didn't. But I like the idea."

"So I dropped by there to see how it had affected their business. And the place was dead. There were no cars, there were no guests."

Filo clapped her hands once. *"Gracias a Dios."*

"Thanks to the Cobras, or whoever did it."

"They must have done it. They must have taken a picture for that purpose."

"Anyway," he continued, "I sat down at a table to have a coffee, and a woman came over and figured that I was there for a girl. So she offered me a girl. In fact, she offered me two girls for the price of one."

"How old were they?"

"About fourteen."

"Well, why do you feel like you did something awful?"

"I wanted to accept the woman's offer."

"But you didn't accept it."

"I almost did."

"No, you didn't," Filo said, shaking her head. "You never would have taken advantage of those girls."

"How do you know?"

"I know you."

"Then you know me better than I do. When she made them lower the tops of their bikinis, I was aroused. She said they'd do anything I wanted, and I imagined— Oh, my God." He slumped into a chair and covered his face with his hands.

"Hey," Filo said gently, laying her hand on the back of his neck. "That woman tempted you, but you didn't yield, and for that you should be proud of yourself."

"I don't feel proud. I feel ashamed."

"For being aroused? Any guy would have been aroused, and in that respect you're like any guy. In fact, it's arrogant to think you're not."

"Arrogant? What do you mean?"

"We all have weaknesses. But God understands that. We're His creatures. So He doesn't blame us for having weaknesses. And He's happy when we overcome them."

Of course he had been taught this since the first grade of Catholic school, but for some reason he always thought it applied to everyone except himself. He began to see that it *was* arrogant not to apply it to himself. "I guess I wouldn't have accepted the offer. And I really wanted to rescue those girls."

"It's a good thing you didn't try. They would have beaten the shit out of you."

"Would they have gotten away with that?"

"They get away with everything. But tell me more about the website."

"I only heard about it. I didn't see it."

"Well, let's look at it. I have a connection to the Internet. I only use it for email, but I can go to websites." She sat down at her computer.

He watched as she activated a browser and did a search.

"There it is. And there *he* is. But I shouldn't be glad to see his picture on their website."

"You shouldn't blame yourself for being glad," he told her, "if I shouldn't blame myself for being aroused."

"You're right," she said, nodding. "And being glad to see his picture on their website isn't the same as condoning what the Cobras did to him."

"I think it's an effective warning to potential customers."

"But they can take that picture off their website."

"And whoever put it there can put it back."

"They must be able to stop things from being put on their website. Otherwise there'd be things like that on every website."

"You mean like pictures of car accidents on the websites of automakers."

"Yeah, things like that."

"Well, let's hope they can't get rid of it."

Filo took a last look at the picture, and then closed the window on the screen.

"Now, what about those girls?" he asked. "How can we rescue them?"

"We can't take them out of that place. We have to wait for them to leave. And we have to persuade them to come with us."

"So tell me how I can help you rescue them."

"The girls sometimes go to the beach. You can watch for them there."

"And what if I see them?"

"Approach them and say you met them. I'm sure they'll remember you. And tell them you have a much better place for them to live."

"Why would they trust me?"

"Because you didn't take advantage of them."

"All right," he said. "I'll watch for them."

"If anyone tries to stop them from going with you, call for help from the guys at the round table. They're always up for a good fight."

Before the wedding his father had replaced Molly as his secretary so that she could be a full-time mother, and when they returned from their honeymoon on Cape Cod his father announced that they had bought a house there. The plan was for Molly and the boys to spend the summer at the Cape, which would give them a chance to get to know each other, while his father would work and go there on weekends.

Because of his mother's illness, the family had never gone anywhere for the summer. They had gone to his father's country club and to the beach at Rye, but that was only for the day. So going to the Cape for the summer was a new experience.

At first his brother didn't like the idea since he would be away from his friends, but it didn't take him long to adapt and find friends on the beach, where they went every day if the weather was nice. They could walk to the beach from their house, and by mid-morning they were in their usual place under an umbrella, with soda and sandwiches in a cooler.

Molly always brought a book with her, but she never did any reading. She had to keep an eye on Gregory, who tirelessly cavorted in the water and gamboled on the sand with his friends. The surf wasn't very dangerous since they were on the bay, but Molly still kept an eye on his brother, taking seriously her new responsibility as a mother.

Ronan never strayed from their place. He sat in his chair and surveyed the scene without ever participating. If a boy or a girl stopped and tried to get him to play, he shook his head and implied that he was somehow disabled.

Molly encouraged him to make friends, but he resisted, unable to imagine anyone wanting to be friends with him.

The big issue that first summer was the fact that he hadn't learned to swim. Gregory had learned in their pool at home, where he played with friends, but Ronan didn't go near the pool because he had a fear of drowning. In fact, he sometimes had nightmares about drowning in which he cried for his mother to save him.

Molly didn't push him, as his father had, but every day she would hold his hand and lead him to the water. It took her a few weeks to get him to advance to a point where the water was up to his shins, and despite her coaxing that was as far as he would go until one day in early July when she got him to advance to a point where the water was up to his knees.

"Now, come toward me," she told him, standing a few feet away from him.

He moved forward an inch or two.

"That's good. You see? It won't hurt you. A little further."

He moved another inch.

"Now, come to me." She stretched out her arms to receive him, extending her hands close enough for him to reach them. "Come on, honey."

"I can't," he said.

"You can. You're almost here."

He leaned forward, moving forward a few more inches, and he clasped her hands.

"You did it. That's great." She drew him toward her and hugged him. "There's nothing to be afraid of. I love you, and I'm here for you."

He let her hug him, but he didn't hug her back. He didn't believe she loved him. She had to say she loved him because she loved his father.

By the end of July he had advanced to a point where the water was up to his mid-thighs. At that point she tried to get him to immerse himself, but he wouldn't do it, even with her holding him with both hands.

"I think you should duck him," he overheard his father tell her one evening. Molly and his father were out on the deck, which overlooked the bay, and Ronan was in the living room lying on the sofa. They evidently didn't know he could overhear their conversation.

"I couldn't do that," Molly said. "It would terrify him."

"It would get him wet," his father said, "and he'd see there's nothing to be afraid of."

"He gets wet when he takes a shower, and that hasn't solved the problem."

"Well, I don't know what the problem is."

"He has a fear of drowning. That's obvious."

"Where did he get it from?"

"I don't know. But he's not the only kid who ever had that fear. My cousin had the same fear when he was little."

"Did he ever learn to swim?"

"He finally did, but it took a long time. So we have to be patient."

"I'm not in any hurry. I just want the kid to have fun."

"I do too. I've never seen him have fun."

Hearing Molly say this had two effects on him. It made him feel sorry for himself, and it made him feel love toward her. He tried to overcome the first effect by remembering how his mother had always told him to think about others, not to think about himself, and he tried to overcome the second effect by imagining how his mother would feel if he started loving anyone else. And he succeeded at overcoming the second effect.

By the end of the summer he had advanced to a point where the water was up to his navel. Molly tried to get him to immerse himself, but he wouldn't do it, even though she was holding him. He imagined going under and never coming up.

The next morning he started watching for Lucy and Elvira at the beach. He had a good view of the beach from the round table, but he couldn't recognize people on the beach from his balcony, so after lunch he lay in a rented lounge chair under the sea grape trees next to Joop's where he could see in both directions. From time to time he would look up from his reading and scan the beach, but he didn't spot either of the girls.

He considered going back to Arabian Nights and asking for them, but he remembered what Filo had said about what would happen if he tried to rescue them from the place, so he kept watching for them and hoping that they would appear.

On Sunday he saw Filo in church with her twenty kids, taking up three pews. He sat in the pew behind them, and he touched a number of small hands while making a sign of peace. He received the host from Daria. He was beginning to feel he belonged in this community, and he could imagine staying here.

The next afternoon he was working in the back office of the clinic when the light suddenly got brighter. This meant that the power was off, and that the inverter had kicked in. The inverter, a system of linked car batteries, stored electricity while the power was on and provided it while the power was off. The inverter had enough capacity to last up to eight hours. At that point if the power hadn't come on again, you had to use candles. The clinic didn't have a generator because Daria didn't want to contribute to the air pollution in the *barrio*.

A few minutes later he heard a commotion outside, and he stopped working in order to listen. Among the sounds of excited people he heard a voice crying: *"Socorro!"*

He got up and opened the door and looked down the hall in time to see Daria rushing out. He went after her, realizing that something had happened outside that needed medical attention. Most likely it was a motorbike accident.

People were surging toward the main street, and Ronan went along with them about fifty feet behind Daria. When she turned at the corner he lost sight of her, but when he got to the main street he saw her pushing her way through a crowd of excited people. As he tried to follow her, he encountered some resistance and even hostility.

"What happened?" he asked the woman next to him.

"A boy was electrocuted," she told him, making a flat statement.

Before he could ask the woman for details the police van came up behind them, and they were separated as they let it pass.

Within minutes the cops were trying to get the people off the street while the detective joined Daria, who was kneeling in a puddle next to a motionless boy.

By then Ronan was close enough to hear them.

"What the hell happened?" Sergio asked her.

"An electric line came loose and fell into the street," Daria told him. "The boy picked it up, and he was standing in this puddle, barefoot."

"Someone must have knocked the line down trying to connect with it."

"That's not what they say. They say the line just came loose."

"You mean it came loose by its own volition?"

"With the lack of maintenance, it doesn't take much for these lines to come loose."

"How old is this kid?" Sergio asked after a silence.

"He just turned seven. I was treating him for bronchitis."

Sergio sighed. "Where's his mother?"

"She's on her way here. She was cleaning a house over on the ridge, and someone went to get her."

"You want her to see her boy like this?"

"I asked someone to bring a blanket. If you'll let me move him, I'll lay him on it."

"If you're ready to certify the cause of death, then you can move him."

"Electrocution, caused by picking up a live wire."

"Why would he try to pick it up?"

"I think he was trying to be helpful. It fell right in the middle of the street."

A woman came forward with a blanket, and Daria carefully lifted the boy and laid him on it. On her knees she prayed: "God our Father, Your power brings us to birth, Your providence guides our lives, and by Your command we return to dust."

Solemnly, she made the sign of the cross.

She was still on her knees when the mother arrived and threw herself on the boy's body, wailing: "*O Pedrito, mi Pedrito!*"

Daria put her hand on the mother's back and held it there until the woman finally sat up, looking dazed. "Your son is with God now."

"I want him here, not in heaven."

"I know, I know."

A woman who could have been the mother's sister knelt down by her and embraced her, relieving Daria, who got up and rejoined the detective.

Ronan waited while she signed a paper, and then he walked back to the clinic with her.

"What's the legal term," Daria asked, "when someone gets killed because something wasn't maintained in working order?"

"Gross negligence," Ronan said.

"Not criminal negligence?"

"I don't know. I'm not an expert on the law."

"Well, whether or not it's criminal negligence, the government is responsible for that boy's death."

"Isn't the plant also responsible?"

"The plant is responsible for generating power. The electric company, which is owned by the government, distributes the power, so they're responsible for maintaining the lines."

"Then why don't they maintain the lines?"

"They say they don't have the money," Daria said. "But they have the money to maintain the lines in rich neighborhoods."

"I guess they could argue that people in those neighborhoods pay for electricity."

"A lot of them don't. They figure they can get away with it, so why pay?"

"Then the electric company has no justification for ignoring the lines in poor neighborhoods."

"It has political justification, but it doesn't have moral justification."

"So what are you going to do about it?" Ronan asked.

"I'm going to file a complaint. And I'm going to ask the town council to pass a resolution for the company to maintain the lines in this neighborhood."

"What about that loose line?"

"They're not in any hurry to repair it."

"Then we should make sure that no one else gets hurt by it."

"No one will," Daria said. "They turned off our power. And they won't turn our power back on until they repair it."

"I guess in the meantime they save money."

"That's why they're in no hurry to repair that line. I hope my inverter lasts long enough. It's hard to examine people by candlelight."

Two days later at ten in the morning the boy's funeral was held at the church, and there wasn't room for all the people who wanted to attend.

Daria assisted Padre Tavarez, and Ronan sat with Filo and her kids, who were all there.

Though Padre Tavarez said the usual comforting words, he was clearly running into an obstacle in people's refusal to accept what had happened. You could sense that in their minds it hadn't been an act of God, but an act of the electric company. And it didn't help that the power was still off and the stores had run out of candles.

Filo's kids rose and held hands as they prayed together: "*Padre nuestro, que estás en cielo, santificado sea tu Nombre—*"

Ronan prayed with them, buoyed by their faith.

When the mass was ended they watched the casket being carried down the aisle, turning as it went by them and sadly gazing after it.

Since she had canceled school that afternoon, Filo invited Ronan to join her and the kids at the beach, so after going home and changing he headed there. Of course, being kids they hadn't taken long to change, and they were already in the water when he got there.

Filo had rented two lounge chairs and was lying in one of them. She was wearing a simple two-piece white bathing suit in which she could have won a prize in a beauty contest if she had cared about such things.

"Hi," she said with a friendly smile.

"Hi," he said, unable to take his eyes off her.

"Would you like to sit down? Or would you like to swim?"

"I think I'll sit down." He had never overcome his fear of drowning, so he hoped to avoid being put to the test.

"They needed this," she said, referring to the kids in the water. "They were very upset by what happened to that boy."

"I can understand. It was very upsetting."

"They were also upset by what happened to that girl. But she didn't have a funeral."

83

"Did they find out who she was?"

"She wasn't anyone, at least in their minds. But the boy had a mother."

"Did he have a father?"

"He had a biological father. But the parents of these kids rarely get married. They have temporary relationships, and they refer to each other as *esposos*, but they don't have legal or religious bonds. And they don't stay together very long."

"Did the father help to support the boy?"

"No, not much. He was typical. He went around impregnating women but never staying with them very long. He had children from at least three women. He kept track of them, and he remembered them on their birthdays."

"Why do the women put up with that?"

"They don't know anything different. Their own fathers were like that, and their father's fathers. It's how men behaved before they started wearing loincloths."

He hesitated, and then he asked: "Was *your* father like that?"

"According to my mother he was. I never knew him."

He waited for her to tell him more, but she lapsed into a silence with her eyes closed.

He scanned the beach, looking for the two girls. He imagined them appearing and joining Filo's kids on the beach. But he didn't see them.

"I'm going for a swim," Filo said, getting up from her chair.

"I'm going to stay here," Ronan said.

"Oh, come on." She found his hand and pulled him upright. She was stronger than you would have guessed.

"I really don't feel like swimming."

"Come on," she said, holding his hand. She reminded him of Molly, as she had from the very beginning, except that she wasn't his stepmother.

Seeing no choice, he went along with her. When they reached the water's edge, the kids began to watch them curiously.

Filo kept going, holding his hand and taking him along with her into the water.

At least the water wasn't as cold as it had been at the Cape.

When the water was up to Ronan's knees he began to feel trepidation, and he would have liked to stop there, but Filo kept going, still holding his hand.

It suddenly occurred to him that she *knew* he was afraid of the water, and that she was going to help him overcome his fear. But how could she have known? How could she have guessed that he had this fear?

The water kept getting deeper, and then suddenly he could no longer touch bottom.

"Trust in God," she told him, letting go of his hand. "He'll hold you up."

He expected to sink like a stone in the water, but something held him up, and he began to move his arms and legs as Molly had instructed him.

Miraculously, he was swimming.

The next morning he was sitting at the round table as usual, having breakfast, when Willem joined them, saying: "Guess what."

"I don't know. What?" Donal said.

"The Cobras have struck again."

"Where?" Hans asked. "What did they do?"

"They killed a guy from the electric company," Willem said, sitting down at the table. "It was one of those guys who go around disconnecting meters."

"If it's the guy who disconnected my meter," Donal said, "he deserved to be killed. I always pay my electric bill, and he cut me off anyway."

"I doubt if it was the same guy," Willem said. "It happened in Puerto Plata."

"How did they kill him?" Hans asked.

"They electrocuted him," Willem said as if they should have guessed. "They caught him disconnecting the meter of a *colmado*, and they held his hands to the contact points."

"They must have been wearing rubber gloves," Hans said.

"They left him at the front entrance of the electric company with a sign on him that said: 'This is what happens to people who let our children get electrocuted.' He was there when the boss came to work this morning."

"I wonder why they chose him," Hans said. "He wasn't involved in maintenance."

"They probably chose him," Donal said, "because he was cutting off the power of a local store. I mean, people won't have any sympathy for him."

"If he has a wife and family, they might. And it was his job to cut off people who don't pay their electric bills."

"They don't know who pays and who doesn't. Before they cut anyone off, at least they should know if he's paying. They shouldn't just guess."

"I wonder if this will have any effect," Willem said.

"It could," Donal said. "It could make them think twice before they cut off anyone's power. But it won't make them maintain the lines in the *barrio*."

"You mean because no one in the *barrio* pays them."

"That's right. It's all about money."

Ronan agreed that it wouldn't make them maintain the lines in the *barrio*, so he was surprised that afternoon when he saw two trucks from the electric company on the main street of the *barrio*. A ladder was leaning against the pole from which the line had fallen, and a guy was up there working at the junction.

People were standing in the street, watching. They must have all known what the Cobras had done, and there was a look of vindication in their eyes.

Inside the clinic he ran into Daria, who followed him to the back office.

"I see they've come to repair the line," Ronan said.

After closing the door Daria said: "I want to believe they came in response to my complaint, or in response to the town council's resolution."

"Maybe they did."

"Did you hear what the Cobras did in Puerto Plata?"

"I heard it this morning at the round table."

"That's why they came. That's what it takes to get those people to do anything."

"Maybe it does. But this time they killed an innocent person."

Daria sighed. "I know. He wasn't a drug dealer or a statutory rapist. He was just a guy doing his job. And he wasn't responsible for the death of that boy."

"So what does that make the Cobras?"

"It makes them terrorists. They're no longer avenging crimes. They're killing innocent people to achieve their goal. And they must believe their goal justifies their method."

"Do you believe it does?"

"No. But it got results," Daria said unhappily. "It made the electric company repair that line."

"I guess it did."

For a while she was silent, and then she said: "I wonder if it's possible to use their method without becoming a terrorist."

"I don't know," Ronan said. "And if you're talking about the power plant, remember what Padre Tavarez asked you. How could you be absolutely sure that there was no one inside the plant when you blew it up?"

"I still don't have an answer to that question. But I'm thinking about it. More and more, I'm thinking about it."

SIX

OVER THE NEXT few days Ronan noticed that business was recovering at Arabian Nights. There were more cars parked on the street and more people in the courtyard. They had removed the dead German from their website, and though they must have lost business from people who had seen him, there were always new people searching the Internet for the service they provided.

The flow of new clients made Ronan all the more anxious to rescue the two girls, so from his vantage point in the lounge chair next to Joop's he kept an eye on the beach, hoping to spot them. And finally, a week after the boy was electrocuted, he did spot them. They had come from behind him and passed within ten feet of him going to the ocean. He hadn't seen their faces, but they were wearing the same bikinis.

Unlike mature women who cautiously walked into the water, they broke into a run and hit the water splashing and shrieking. Within a few minutes they were over their heads, swimming and bobbing in the long swells.

Seeing an opportunity, he got up and went to the water, and using his new ability to swim, he headed toward them. With their hair sleeked back, they looked like a pair of otters.

"*Hola,*" he said, approaching them.

"*Hola,*" they said, almost together. They exchanged a look with each other, indicating that they remembered him.

"Which one of you is Lucy?"

"I'm Lucy," the girl with gray eyes said fearlessly.

"Then you must be Elvira," he said, turning to the other girl.

"I am. What's your name?"

"I'm Ronan," he said.

They giggled as if that was a funny name.

"Do you remember me?"

They nodded together.

"Well, I remember you," he said. "I've been waiting for a chance to talk with you. And this seems like a good place to talk."

"It is," Lucy said. "No one can hear us."

"Do you go to school?"

"No, we're not allowed to."

"When was the last time you went to school?"

Lucy considered. "About two years ago."

"Would you like to go to school?"

"Yes. I miss school."

"I do too," Elvira said. "I miss playing with other kids."

"I can get you back in school," he said. "And I can find you a place to live."

"What kind of place?" Lucy asked doubtfully.

"A place where you can be kids again."

"Is it a foster home?"

"No. It's a boarding school."

"What's that?"

"A school where you live in a dormitory."

"Are there other kids to play with?" Elvira asked.

"There are twenty other kids—girls and boys."

"I don't want to play with boys. I only want to play with girls."

"You can play with whoever you like."

"Who will take care of us?" Lucky asked.

"A very nice woman."

"That's what they said about Vilma."

"Who's Vilma?" he asked, though he could guess.

"The bitch who offered you two of us for the price of one."

"Well, this woman is the opposite of Vilma."

"Is she your wife?"

"No. She's a friend."

"You're not from here."

"I'm from New York."

"Are you a cop?"

"No, I'm a teacher."

"If we go to that school, will you be our teacher?" Elvira asked.

He hadn't thought about it, but coming from this girl it didn't seem like a bad idea. "Yeah, I could be one of your teachers."

"Give us a minute," Lucy told him.

He waited while they swam away and had a conference, talking earnestly and making gestures only with their heads since they needed their arms to stay afloat.

When they came back Lucy said: "We want to go to that school and live there, but we have a problem. They won't let us leave Arabian Nights."

"You've left. You're here."

"Our clothes are there."

"We'll buy you new clothes. You don't have to go back there for anything."

"You'll buy us new clothes?" Lucy asked.

"Whatever you need," Ronan said, willing to bribe them.

The girls exchanged another look with each other, and then almost in unison said: "All right. We'll go with you."

Their willingness to take a chance with him made him feel responsible for them. It also made him realize how easy it was to lure kids into places like Arabian Nights.

As they waded out of the water anyone watching them might have assumed that he was a father with his two daughters. But from the way the girls looked around, he could tell they had another thought in mind—that someone from Arabian Nights would stop them.

"Come on," he said, taking each of them by the hand. "It's not far."

Leaving his book on the lounge chair, he led them through Joop's and past the round table. He remembered the advice from Filo to ask the guys at the table for help if anyone tried to stop him, so he wanted them to see him with the girls.

They could have made comments, but they didn't.

The girls held his hands as if they were afraid to let go, and from time to time Lucy glanced back over her shoulder to make sure that no one was following them.

"How old are the kids in this school?" she asked.

"They're around your age. Some are older, and some are younger."

"You know, we're fourteen."

"We're not fourteen," Elvira said.

"We're supposed to say we're eighteen."

"No one would believe it, except the police."

"How old *are* you?" Ronan asked.

"I'm thirteen," Elvira said.

"I'm thirteen and a half," Lucy said.

"How long have you been at Arabian Nights?"

"About six months. It seems like forever."

Ronan understood that by rescuing the girls he was trying to redeem himself for being aroused by them, but in talking with them he realized that he wasn't *only* trying to do that. He was also trying to help them start a new life.

"Would you buy us something to drink?" Lucy asked as they approached a *colmado*.

"Sure," he said. He steered them inside, where they let go of his hands and went to the cooler.

They peered through the glass and found what they were looking for. Lucy opened the door of the cooler and got out two bottles of chocolate milk.

He was taking the bottles to the counter when Elvira spotted a kitten on the floor.

"Oh, look," she said to Lucy, pointing to it.

The kitten, a little ball of orange fuzz, stared at them with enormous eyes.

Elvira picked it up and cuddled it, rubbing her cheek against it, while Lucy stroked it.

"Her name is Mina," the guy behind the counter told them.

"She's so cute," Elvira said.

"She's adorable," Lucy said.

"She's two weeks old," the guy said.

"Oh, the little baby," Elvira said, mothering the kitten.

"Can we come back and see her?" Lucy asked.

"Sure," Ronan said, paying for the drinks.

As they left the *colmado* the girls took his hands again, holding the bottles in their free hands and tilting back their heads to drink.

By now Lucy had stopped glancing back over her shoulder.

The girls talked about the kitten, which for now had become their main interest.

When they reached the center Filo gave them a warm welcome and produced two big fluffy towels, which she wrapped around them comfortingly.

"They don't have any clothes," he told her.

"We have clothes for them," she said. "And tomorrow we'll buy them new clothes."

"I promised them we would."

Filo gave him a look as if to say: "If that's all it took to get them to come here, you did well."

He did feel he had done well. In fact, it was a long time since he had felt that way.

"Are you hungry?" Filo asked them.

They hesitated as if they didn't know how to respond.

"If you are, I can make a sandwich for you. Would you like a sandwich?"

"I would," Lucy finally said.

"I would too," Elvira said.

"I have to leave," Ronan told the girls. "I'll be back tomorrow."

"You're still going to be our teacher, aren't you?" Elvira said.

"Yes," he said with a look at Filo.

"He's going to teach you English," Filo said.

"We know some English," Lucy said.

"Yeah, I can imagine," Filo said. "Ronan's going to teach you other things to say."

"I'm also going to teach you to read English." Impulsively, he gave each girl a kiss on the forehead. "I'll see you tomorrow."

Walking back to his apartment he thought about Amy, who had been around the same age as Lucy and Elvira when she forced the issue.

Amy lived across the street, and they had been friends since kindergarten. The oldest of five children, Amy was a tomboy, and despite her mother's objections she had her black hair cut short and she wore jeans instead of dresses. Since they were lost in the middle of the gender spectrum, Amy and Ronan naturally gravitated toward each other, avoiding both the world of boys and the world of girls.

When they were in second grade they devised a system that enabled them to communicate with each other at night. From their bedrooms at the front of their respective houses they spelled out words in Morse code using flashlights. Their messages were usually about arranging times and places for them to get together.

By the time they started high school the kids their age were preoccupied with sex. Ronan and Amy talked about sex, but they agreed that it wasn't for them, and they continued doing what they had always done, which consisted mainly of hanging out.

Concerned about Amy's total lack of social life, her mother organized a party to which she invited the kids their age who lived in the neighborhood. The party was held in the basement of Amy's house, where there was a large finished room with a bar, an entertainment center, sofas and chairs, and a parquet floor.

Amy resisted having the party, and as soon as her mother had gone upstairs she slipped out the basement door with Ronan. They wandered over to Sunnybrook Park, where they hung out until they were sure that the party was over.

When they returned, Amy's mother was waiting for them.

"Where have you been?" her mother asked, looking very angry.

"We went out for a breath of fresh air."

"Don't lie to me. You've been gone all evening."

"Well, I didn't want to have a party."

"You were the hostess. You were supposed to entertain your guests."

"How? By taking off my clothes?"

"Don't get fresh with me, young lady."

"So how was I supposed to entertain them?"

"By talking with the girls, by dancing with the boys."

"I don't like talking with girls," Amy retorted. "And I don't like dancing with boys. I like hanging out with Ronan."

"What do you do with him?" her mother asked suspiciously.

"We just hang out. You think we have sex?"

"I have no idea what you do, but for what you did tonight you're grounded."

"What does that mean?"

"It means you can't see Ronan."

"For how long?"

"For as long as I say." Her mother turned to him and said: "You understand? If you don't stay away from her, I'll tell your mother."

It really wasn't much of a threat since Molly had her hands full with her three daughters.

"You understand?"

"Yeah, I understand."

"Then go home and stay away from her."

He exchanged a look with Amy, and then he went out the basement door.

When he got home they communicated using the flashlights. They arranged to meet at one o'clock in the morning outside the basement door of Amy's house.

They were all asleep in his house when he crept downstairs. Without making a sound he went out the front door and crossed the street and walked around to Amy's backyard.

The basement door was open, and she was standing just outside. There wasn't a light on, but he could see her face, and it looked different. For a moment he thought she was someone else, and he wondered if her mother had set a trap for him.

"Come in," she said in her usual voice.

He went into the basement, and she closed the door.

"I don't want to turn on a light," she told him.

"That's all right. I can see you in the dark."

"I like meeting in secret, don't you?"

"Yeah," he said. But a fear was rising from deep within him, and it wasn't the fear that they would be caught.

"So what would you like to do?" she asked.

"Oh, I don't know," he said. Without light their options were rather limited.

"I'd like to sit on the sofa."

"Okay." He followed her and sat down next to her.

"My mother doesn't understand how we can just hang out together."

"I guess she thinks we're up to no good."

"She thinks we're having sex," Amy said. "You know when a teacher thinks you're talking in class and you're not? It makes you *want* to talk in class."

He saw where she was going with this, and he didn't know how to respond.

"I'm not saying I want to have sex because my mother thinks we're having it. But maybe we should try kissing."

"Kissing?" he said, the fear rising.

"That's what people do when they like each other."

"I guess they do. Have you ever kissed a boy?"

"No. I mean, not on the mouth. I've kissed my brothers on the cheek."

"I've kissed my sisters on the cheek, but I've never kissed anyone on the mouth."

"Then we should learn to kiss that way."

By now the fear was rising from his stomach. It was like the fear that had stopped him from immersing himself in the ocean.

"Come on," she urged him, leaning toward him.

"I can't," he said, holding back.

"I thought you liked me."

"I do like you."

"Then why won't you kiss me?"

"I don't know how."

"You can learn if you try."

He didn't want to, but he didn't see any way out of it. "Okay. I'll try."

Clumsily, she put her arm around his neck and pressed her mouth against his.

With the fear now risen up to his throat he suddenly panicked and pushed her away.

"Why did you do that?" she asked, sounding hurt.

"I don't know. I couldn't help it."

"You don't like me."

"I do like you. I'm just not ready to kiss you."

"Well, let me know when you're ready," she said, getting up from the sofa.

"I'm sorry," he said, feeling that he had really blown it.

"I'm sorry too." She went to the door and opened it for him.

Before going out he paused and said: "I *do* like you."

"No, you don't." She had tears in her eyes. "If you did, you wouldn't have pushed me away."

He had never seen her cry before, and as she closed the door he wondered what had happened to his friend Amy.

After that his mother didn't have to stop them from seeing each other.

He was getting ready to walk to the clinic when there was knock on the door. He assumed it was Janos with a plumber to fix the leak in the bathroom sink.

But it was the detective who had questioned Filo.

"I'm sorry to disturb you," Sergio said, "but I'd like to ask you some questions."

"About what?" he asked, having no idea.

"About two girls who were reported missing."

"Which girls do you mean?"

"Lucy and Elvira."

"Come in," Ronan said, opening the door the rest of the way.

"You have a great view of the ocean," Sergio said, looking out the window.

"Who reported them missing?"

"The manager of Arabian Nights. She said they took a break and never returned."

"Well, why are you asking *me* about them?"

"You were seen with them."

"You can look around, but you won't find them here."

"I didn't expect to find them here."

"If you think you know where they are, then why don't you go there?"

"I will go there, but I wanted to talk with you first."

Sergio was standing with his back to the window, and Ronan was standing near the door that led out to the balcony. "Would you like to go outside and sit down?"

"Yeah, that's a good idea."

He held the door while Sergio went out.

"You have a great view of the mountain too."

At that moment the clouds had parted, and the statue of Christ loomed over them.

"It helps me do the right thing."

Sergio smiled. "We all need something that helps us do the right thing. But it's not always easy to know what the right thing is."

"It's easy in this case."

"You think it is?" Sergio asked, sitting down.

"Why isn't it?" Ronan asked, taking the other chair.

"It's a complicated situation. For one thing, the owners of Arabian Nights have a lot of friends, and Filomena has a lot of enemies."

"That doesn't make the owners right and Filomena wrong."

"It doesn't. We've come a long way from the days when might made right. But it still helps to have powerful friends."

"Can the powerful friends of the owners force those girls back into slavery?"

"They weren't slaves," Sergio said, shaking his head. "They were employees, and they were paid for the work they did."

"They didn't choose to work there."

"They did. They're legal age."

"They're not legal age. They're only thirteen."

"The manager has papers that say they're eighteen."

"And you believe what those papers say?"

97

"They're legal documents."

"Have you ever *looked* at those girls?"

"No. I've never laid eyes on them."

"When you go and question Filomena, take a good look at them. You'll see for yourself that they're not eighteen."

"You have to understand," Sergio told him, shifting in his chair, "my job is to protect those girls. And I know you believe that by taking them to Filomena you've put them in a safe place. But it's not a safe place. It's a dangerous place where kids are indoctrinated into a cult."

"A cult?" He laughed. "Where did you get that idea?"

"It's common knowledge. If you think about it, her group has all the attributes of a cult. She's a charismatic leader who gives them unconditional love, acceptance, and attention. She also gives them a new identity."

"You could say that about the pastor of a church."

"Yeah, I could say that about the pastor who persuaded his followers to commit mass suicide by drinking Kool Aid laced with cyanide."

"She doesn't use the methods of a cult leader. She doesn't brainwash those kids. She runs a school where they learn the skills they need in the world."

"From what I've seen, those kids act like members of a cult."

"They act like members of a church. Do you have something against churches?"

"No. I don't," Sergio said, "though I was brainwashed at a Catholic school."

"A lot of us were brainwashed at Catholic schools, but we're not members of a cult."

"Sometimes I wonder. But she goes beyond what they do at those schools. She turns them into followers of Filomena."

"Would you rather have them be followers of Vilma?"

"Vilma?" Sergio looked blank "You mean the woman who manages Arabian Nights?"

"Yeah, the woman with a nose like a parrot. Is she also one of the owners?"

"No, she's only the manager."

"Then who are the owners?"

"You don't need to know."

He took this remark as meaning that it would be better for him if he didn't know. "Can I ask you something?"

"Sure. Go ahead."

"Did you come here to pursue an investigation, or did you come here to warn me?"

"I came here to do both," Sergio said. "If you're smart, you'll take those girls back to Arabian Nights, and you won't interfere with their business again."

"Since you've been honest with me," Ronan said, "I'll be honest with you. I'm not smart. So you'll have to protect me as well as those girls."

"There are limits on how much I can protect you."

"I understand. We all have limits."

The warning from the detective didn't have the intended effect on him. Like the warning issued by Amy's mother, it made him aware of the risk he was taking but at the same time it made him want to defy it.

He shared his feelings with Filo the next morning. As soon as they were in the privacy of the back office he asked: "Did Sergio come here yesterday?"

"Oh, yes," Filo said. "He came here to see if I was holding those girls captive."

Ronan smiled. "What did you tell him?"

"I told him they came here by their own volition."

Ronan sat down, ignoring the pile of papers on the table. "I did talk them into it, but Sergio thinks I recruited them to join your cult."

"He doesn't think that," Filo said, sitting down. "He's just saying what people have told him."

"You mean the people we rescued them from?"

"Yeah, they'll say anything to ruin my reputation. They even say we involve the kids in satanic rituals."

"Why does he listen to them?"

"He has to listen to people who have a lot of influence."

"I guess he does if he wants to keep his job."

"Eventually he has to separate the facts from the fantasies," Filo said, "and I believe he'll be able to do that—if they don't interfere with him."

"Who would interfere with him?"

"People at a high level."

"Do they have an interest in the business?"

"Maybe not an ownership interest, but it provides them with a steady stream of income."

"He gave me a warning," Ronan said after a moment. "He told me that if I was smart, I'd take those girls back to Arabian Nights."

"What did you tell him?"

"I told him I'm not smart."

"Good for you," she said with a look of admiration. "But I wouldn't take his warning lightly. You could get hurt."

"I understand. And I understand that he can give me only limited protection."

Filo considered. "I think it was a friendly warning. Sergio doesn't like to see people get hurt. He also doesn't like it to happen on his watch."

"And his solution is for me to take the girls back?"

"For him it's an easy solution. It prevents the kind of violence that goes on record."

"You mean what happens to the girls who work there doesn't go on record?"

"Not unless a girl gets killed. And even then if the girl's no one, it doesn't remain long in the public consciousness."

"What if she's the daughter of someone at a high level?"

"That would be different. But there was a time not long ago when even people at a high level couldn't protect their daughters from sexual predation."

"What happened to them?" Ronan asked.

"We had a dictator who liked to have sex with underage girls. If he saw an attractive girl, he would send a guy to her father to ask for her. If the father refused, he was arrested and thrown into prison and tortured. Meanwhile the dictator had already seized the girl and used her for his pleasure."

"Are you talking about Trujillo?"

She nodded. "Rafael Leonidas Trujillo Molina. He ruled our country for more than thirty years, and whatever his admirers claim, the guy was a monster."

"How old were the girls?"

"The same age as Lucy and Elvira, and even younger."

"Then he would have liked Arabian Nights."

"He didn't have to go to places like that. He used his power to get what he wanted."

"From what you're saying," Ronan said after thinking about it, "the only thing that's changed is that now people at a high level don't have to worry about their daughters."

"They don't have to worry about their daughters being seized and raped by a dictator. But if they're not at a high level, they do have to worry about their daughters. For poor people," Filo said bleakly, "nothing has changed."

He was silent in respect for her assessment of the situation.

"Come on," she said, getting up from her chair. "I need to go out and see the world that God created for us."

She led him out of the building and down the street and beyond the pastures to the base of the mountain that rose at the far end of the beach. They went single file up a path that wound around the mountain. The path evidently wasn't used much, and if you hadn't known it was there, you might not have found it.

When they reached the top they sat down on a long rock that made a perfect bench. From there you had a view of the ocean, the beach, the town, and the mountain with the statue of Christ on top. At that moment He was hidden by clouds.

"I come here to nourish my soul," Filo told him. "I can see the world, but I can't see the ugly details. And I can't hear the cries of pain."

"You can't hear anything," Ronan observed. "Not even the ocean."

"When there's more wind, you can hear it. But then you can't hear anything else."

They sat there enjoying the silence.

"I always tell the girls they should talk about what hurts them. And for a change I'm going to follow my own advice."

He waited for her to continue.

"I never knew my biological father. I assume he was a tourist, and that he was Irish. People tell me I look Irish."

"You do," he said. "And I should know."

"Are you Irish?"

"A hundred percent."

"Well, as you can see, I'm not a hundred percent Irish. I'm half Irish and half Dominican. I have my father's blond hair and blue eyes, but I have my mother's brown skin."

He refrained from telling her how beautiful she was.

"I imagine that my father had a fling with my mother and then went home without knowing he had made my mother pregnant. She had a baby girl, and for a while she took care of it. But she was poor, and she developed a drug habit, so when the girl was around ten she sold her. She must have gotten a lot of money for a girl with blond hair and blue eyes."

His heart ached as he listened to her story.

"The girl spent the next four years in a place like Arabian Nights. She did whatever they told her to do. She didn't know any other way of life. And then one day a young priest came into the place. When he saw her standing with the older girls he gently took her hand and led her out. They didn't stop him because he was a priest. He got a taxi and had it drive them to a convent, where she lived for the next six years, going to school and helping the nuns. She started the process of becoming a nun, but then she realized what her mission was, so she left the convent with the blessing of the nuns and pursued her mission."

"Where was the convent?"

"In Santo Domingo," Filo said. "I heard there was a woman in Sosua doing what I wanted to do, so I got on a bus and came north. I worked with her for several years, and then I had an opportunity to open a center here."

"When was that?"

"Almost three years ago. I met Daria, and she helped me find some donors."

"So you started your center about a year after Daria built her clinic in the *barrio.*"

"Yes. And we've been helping each other since then."

"Was your name always Filomena?"

"No. I took that name in the convent. Filomena was an early Christian martyr. She was the daughter of a Greek king who had converted to Christianity. At the age of thirteen she took a vow of chastity. When the emperor threatened to make war on her father, he went to Rome with his family to ask for peace. The emperor fell in love with Filomena, who was about fourteen at the time. She refused to marry him, so he tortured her with scourging, drowning, and being shot with arrows. With the help of angels she survived those torments and still refused to marry the emperor, so he had her decapitated."

"He sounds like Trujillo."

Filo nodded. "He *was* like Trujillo. Men with that kind of power are all alike."

"Why did you take the name of Filomena?"

"We have a lot in common," she said. "I'm not a saint like her, but she's my model."

"Did you take a vow of chastity?"

"Yes. But for me it wasn't much of a sacrifice. After all the things they made me do, I have no desire to have sex. And for me there wouldn't be any point in having sex. I can't have children. I got a disease from one of those men, and to save their valuable property they removed my reproductive system."

"I'm sorry," he said, reaching for her hand.

"I'm sorry too. I would have liked to have children." She took a deep breath and let it out. "So there. I followed my advice. I talked about what hurts me."

"I'm glad you did. I was beginning to envy you."

103

"Why would you envy me?"

"You're beautiful, you're nice, and you have a mission."

"You're attractive, and you're nice."

"You left out one thing."

"That you don't have a mission?"

"Yeah, how did you know?"

"If you did," she said kindly, "you wouldn't be on a leave of absence."

"I guess I wouldn't."

"But I have a feeling you'll find a mission."

"You do?" In appreciation he lifted her hand and kissed it.

"Oh, look," she said with her eyes on the mountain.

The clouds had parted, and the arms of Christ the Redeemer stretched out toward them in a gesture of infinite understanding.

It didn't take them long. When he reached the last landing of the stairs going up to his apartment he saw a guy standing at the top, a big guy in a tank top and basketball shorts. The guy smiled at him menacingly.

He turned, with the idea that he could escape by running back down, but he saw another big guy on the stairs below him.

They had him trapped.

Ronan had been in fights as a kid, and he had won some of them, but the odds in the present situation didn't look good. He was outnumbered, the guys were big, and they both had machetes, which they brandished expertly.

"What do you want?" he asked the guy at the top of stairs. It was possible that they had come here only to rob him.

"We want to hurt you," the guy said.

"You don't even know me."

"We know what you did."

"What did I do?"

"You stole property."

"I think you have the wrong guy."

"We have the right guy."

"Well, hurting me won't accomplish anything. It'll only get you into trouble."

"We don't have to worry about getting into trouble."

"I think you do." He figured that if he could keep them talking, then someone might come along and help him. "The police are protecting me."

That got a laugh from the guy below.

"The police don't care what happens to you," the guy above said as if he had inside information.

"Well, *I* care what happens to him," a deep voice said.

Ronan turned and saw Janos on the landing below with an assault rifle like the ones the guerrillas in Colombia had used.

"He's my tenant. Now, drop those machetes or I'll blow your *kibaszott* heads off."

The guy below looked for instructions from the guy above.

"Drop it," Janos said, aiming the rifle at him. "Under the law I have a right to kill you, and you won't be the first people I killed."

Ronan believed him, remembering what Donal had said about the expatriates, and the guy at the top of stairs evidently believed him because he dropped his machete.

"Kick it down the stairs."

The guy kicked the machete down the stairs, and Ronan immediately picked it up.

"You too," Janos told the guy below. "Drop it, or I'll blow your head off."

The guy did as he was told.

"Now, step back so that this gentleman can get by you. Turn around, and face the wall. Raise your hands over your head."

When the guy had complied Ronan slipped past him and joined Janos on the landing.

"Here," Janos said, handing him a cell phone. "I'm not good at doing more than one thing at a time. What do you call it?"

"Multitasking."

"Whatever. Call the police. The number's in there."

Ronan found the number and pressed the green button to make the call.

"We didn't touch him," the guy at the top of the stairs said.

"You would have if I hadn't stopped you."

"We were only trying to scare him."

"Whatever you were trying to do," Janos said, "you committed the crime of attempted assault, and you'll spend time in prison for that."

The guy said nothing, looking unhappy. He was probably thinking about how his employers would react when they found out he had botched the job.

"Now, go up and join your buddy," Janos told the guy on the stairs. "I want you together so that if I have to fire, I can kill you both with one shot."

While they waited for the police to arrive, Janos talked about a toilet he had to replace in one of the apartments. Over the years the minerals in the hard water had accumulated in the flush passage until they had almost closed it, like the fat deposits in an artery, and there was no way to clear it out.

The guys who had come to hurt Ronan didn't show any interest in the problem.

Sergio finally came up the stairs followed by two men in uniform. When he heard what had happened he looked at Ronan as if to say: "I warned you."

As he watched the police take the two guys away Ronan wondered what their employer would do next.

SEVEN

THE POWER WENT off that evening before he finished cleaning up the kitchen, so he left the pasta pot in the sink and used a flashlight to pour a glass of rum and get a cigar and find his way through the living room and out onto the balcony.

There was no light from the moon or stars, but there were lights in some of the buildings down below. He could hear the sound of generators, which ruined the peace of the evening, and he missed the silence he had enjoyed with Filo on top of the mountain.

He smoked the cigar and sipped the rum and waited for the lights to come on, but they were still off when he went to bed.

The next morning he took his usual walk on the beach, conscious of the possibility that the owners of Arabian Nights would send more goons after him, though he doubted they would since even at that hour the beach was a public place. Most likely they were rethinking their strategy to recover the girls. Still, he didn't take any foolish chances.

Later that morning he met with Lucy and Elvira in a classroom in order to assess their level of English. They were wearing new clothes—capris and tee shirts that said "Life is good." They had flip-flops on their feet.

The girls sat together across from him at a table that rocked when you leaned on it, so they spent a little time folding a piece of cardboard and putting it under one of the legs.

"What's your name?" he asked Lucy in English.

"I call myself Lucy," the girl said, literally translating the Spanish idiom.

"In English you say my name is Lucy."

Elvira giggled. "Your name is not Lucy."

"No, *my* name is Ronan."

"His name is Ronan," Elvira said.

"That's good. Now, what's her name?"

"Her name is Lucy."

"What's *her* name?" he asked Lucy.

"Her name is Elvira," Lucy said.

"Good. And what's your name?"

"My name is Lucy. But can I change it?"

"Why do you want to change it?"

"It is not my name."

"It's not? What *is* your name?"

"My name is Lourdes."

"My name is Encarnación," Elvira said.

"They are not the names of *putas*," Lucy said. "So they change our names."

"Well, at least they didn't change the first letters of your names. Do you want to go back to your old names?"

"No. I want a new name."

"I do too," Elvira said. "Will you give us new names?"

"I think you should choose your own names," Ronan said. "And maybe I can get a list of names for you to choose from. Would that help?"

The girls nodded.

"So let's continue. How old are you?"

"I have thirteen and a half years," Lucy said.

"In English you say I'm thirteen and a half."

"I am thirteen and a half," Lucy repeated.

"I am thirteen," Elvira said.

"Good. What's this?" Ronan asked them, patting himself on top of the head.

"Hairs," Lucy said.

"In English you say hair."

"Do you say come hair?" Elvira asked.

"No, you say come heeere."

"Come heeere," Elvira repeated.

They went through the parts of the body, avoiding those parts that might elicit giggles.

"One foot, two feet," he told them.

They repeated it, lifting their feet to the height of the table.

"Do you want us to tell you the words we learn at Arabian Nights?" Lucy asked.

"No, I don't think so," Ronan said.

"But what if they are bad words?"

"If you say a bad word, I'll let you know."

"Remember the kitten we saw at the *colmado?*"

"Her name is Mina," Elvira said.

"Can I call Mina a pussy?"

"Yes. She's a pussycat."

"That is not a bad word?"

"It's a bad word when it refers to a part of the body."

The girls giggled, exchanging a look.

"So if I want to say a kitten," Lucy said, "I can use that word. But if I want to say a part of the body, I cannot use it."

"That's right," Ronan told her. "You said that perfectly in English."

"We hear much English at that place," Elvira said.

"And much German," Lucy said. "Is *ficken* a bad word?"

"Yeah, it is," Ronan said, imagining how they had learned it. "So you shouldn't use it."

When he left them and joined Filo in her office she asked: "How did it go?"

"I think it went well. I have an idea of where they are."

"We have books in the library that you can use."

"Do you have a book of Spanish names?"

"I have a list of Spanish names that I got from the Internet."

"They want to change their names."

"I know. They always do."

"Why don't they go back to their old names?"

"Because they also have bad memories of their lives before they were enslaved."

"Lourdes and Encarnación," Ronan said, reflecting. "They are not the names of *putas.*"

Filo grimaced. "That sounds like Lucy."

"Yeah, those are her words."

"Well, the girl's right. They're not the names of *putas.*"

"What was your original name?"

"María Altagracia."

"I have a question. If your mothers were going to sell you into sex slavery, why did they give you names like Lourdes, Encarnación, and María Altagracia?"

"When we were born they didn't plan to sell us."

"They hoped you would be saints?"

"Or at least good girls."

"Elvira asked if I would give them new names. I told her they should choose their own names. So if you give them that list, they can start working on it."

"Okay, I'll give the list to them. I always wonder what names they'll choose. And I never guess."

"My only guess is that they'll choose names with the same first letters."

"Well, let's see," Filo said as if she would be happy with whatever names they chose.

The generators were still running as Ronan walked to the clinic that afternoon. He figured that the power had been off for about twenty hours, and he wondered if by now the people who used inverters were out of power.

That question was answered when he got to the clinic and found that there was no power. By the daylight that came through the windows you could see your way around, but you couldn't see anything closely. And of course you couldn't use the computer.

Daria joined him in the back office, taking a break.

"What's happening?" he asked her.

"They shut down the plant because the government owes them money."

"I thought the government always owed them money."

"It always does. But it owes them even more money now."

"Well, what if the government can't find the money to pay them?"

"That's a good question. And I don't know the answer. The government and the power plant are playing politics. The government blames the power plant, and the power plant blames the government. And the people blame them both."

"What are the effects here?"

"The worst effect is the lack of water. We get our water from a cistern on the hill," Daria explained. "The city pumps water into the cistern, and water flows down into the *barrio* by the force of gravity. The cistern has enough water to last a day. So if the city doesn't keep pumping water into it, the *barrio* runs out of water."

"Doesn't the city have generators for that purpose?"

"Oh, yes. But in long outages the generators break down, so then they have to ration the water. And guess where it goes."

"To people in the city?"

She nodded. "Yes. And to people in the rich neighborhood of Santa Cruz. The last place it goes is into our cistern."

"What's the situation now?"

"We're almost out of water. And what's left will go fast since people have begun to hoard it."

"What will happen if the water runs out?"

"People won't be able to bathe or flush their toilets or wash their dishes or wash their clothes. And they won't have water to drink."

"You can't live long without water."

"No. You can't. The water we get from the city isn't good. It's full of infectious bacteria that shorten people's lives. But it's better than no water."

"Is there any other way you can get water?" Ronan asked.

"We can buy it from a company, which will bring it by truck. And that'll keep us going for a while, but if this outage doesn't end soon then they won't have any water for us. They'll sell it to the highest bidder."

"People must be getting angry."

"They *are* getting angry, and I am too. I feel like grabbing one

111

of those white men in suits and sticking his head into a toilet full of shit."

He didn't blame her.

The power was still off when he got up the next morning. By then he figured that it had been off for about thirty-five hours. He still heard generators but fewer of them. Presumably, some had broken down and others had run out of fuel.

After his walk on the beach he sat down at the round table with the usual guys.

"I can only give you bread for breakfast," Joop told him.

"That's okay. You don't have coffee?"

"I don't have water."

"Have a beer," Hans said. "It's warm, but it's still Presidente."

"There's nothing wrong with warm beer," Donal said. "We drink it all the time."

"That isn't beer. It's dog piss."

"I'll have a Presidente," Ronan told Joop.

At that moment Willem arrived, saying: "Guess what."

"Whenever you say that," Donal said, "I know that something terrible has happened."

"We don't feel like guessing," Hans said. "Tell us."

"There were protests in Santiago—"

"We already knew that," Hans said. "The people are finally protesting again the outages."

"What you may not know," Willem said, "is that the police fired at a crowd of protesters and killed a fourteen-year-old boy."

"Why did they fire at the protesters?" Ronan asked.

"I don't know. Maybe someone threw a stone at them."

"That's what protesters do," Hans said, "when the police try to break them up. And then the police fire at them. It happens everywhere."

"What did the protesters do," Ronan asked, "after the police fired at them?"

"They dispersed and went away," Willem said, "but then they came back in a bigger crowd and marched on city hall."

"Well, maybe the politicians will pay attention to them," Donal said.

"Why should they pay attention," Hans asked, "to people who have no money or influence?"

"That's what the king and queen of France asked when the people marched on them. And look what happened to them."

"They wouldn't have a revolution here."

"They would have had one in the sixties if the Americans hadn't sent in the marines."

"If things get out of control," Willem asked, "do you think your country will do that again?"

"We might send in the marines," Ronan said. "We never learn from our mistakes."

"It would be cheaper," Donal said, "for your country to lend money to the government so it could pay the power plants."

"The government's responsible for that boy's death," Hans said. "It's their fault we don't have power."

"It's not their job to generate power," Willem said. "It's the job of the private companies. So they're responsible."

For a while they argued over who was responsible for the boy's death, and finally Donal said: "Well, it doesn't matter what we think. What matters is what the Cobras think."

Following in his brother's footsteps, he went to Fordham University, but whereas his brother had majored in business, Ronan majored in English. His father thought it was a useless major, but Molly argued that it was a good major for someone who wanted to be a teacher, though that wasn't what his father had in mind for him.

Like most Fordham students he lived at home and commuted to the Bronx campus, driving the car that his father had given him when he graduated from Fordham Prep. He didn't play sports and he didn't join clubs, and being on campus only for his classes he didn't have any social life there. After class he came home and studied, and he got good grades. In fact, he always made the dean's list beginning with his first semester.

Molly kept trying to put him together with other kids his age, but she had no more success at that than she had at teaching him to swim. He had little interest in the things girls did or talked about, and he had even less interest in the things boys did or talked about. He loved reading, and he immersed himself not only in the novels, plays, and poems that were assigned in his courses but also in other works by the same authors. By his junior year he was writing poems, though he never showed them to anyone. He wrote a lot about love and death, which for him were interchangeable.

In the spring of his senior year he met Lyle, a fellow student in the seminar on modern poetry. Lyle was a blond, blue-eyed boy who really seemed to understand the complex poems they were reading. When he made a good comment the other students treated him as an upstart, and when he made an especially good comment the professor treated him as an upstart. But Ronan was impressed, and he was glad to have found a boy who talked about things he could relate to. It wasn't long before they were joining each other in discussions, supporting and expanding each other's analyses of the poems.

As they left the seminar room one day Lyle suggested that they have coffee together, and since Ronan didn't have any more classes that day he welcomed the idea.

Instead of going to the student center, Lyle led him off campus to a place where arty students hung out. They sat at a table and ordered espressos.

"You know," Lyle told him, "you're the only other person in our class who understands the poems."

"I like reading poems," Ronan said. He wouldn't have admitted this to other guys, but he was comfortable in saying it to Lyle.

"Who's your favorite modern poet?"

"I don't know. I like Eliot, and I like Yeats—"

"Have you read Dylan Thomas?"

"Oh, yeah. I like him too."

"Have you read Hart Crane?"

"No. I haven't. But I saw him on the list."

"He's my favorite modern poet."

"What does he write about?"

"His feelings. I mean, all poets write about their feelings, but Hart Crane writes about feelings that other poets don't write about."

"I'll read him in advance."

"The thing to read is 'Voyages.' It's not assigned. It was probably censored."

Ronan's interest was aroused. The censorship policy of the Jesuits, who ran Fordham, was less strict than the policy of the Church as a whole, so if they had censored this poem then it was about something forbidden.

"Do you live at home?" Lyle asked as they sipped their coffee.

"Yeah," Ronan said. "But we have a big house, so I have a lot of freedom."

"You don't have as much freedom as you'd have if you lived in an apartment."

"Do you live in an apartment?"

"I live a block away from here. I lived in the dorm for two years, but I finally got out of there. It was almost as bad as living at home."

"Where are you from?"

"Scarsdale," Lyle said as if he wasn't proud of it.

"So you're not far away from home."

"Geographically I'm not far away, but mentally I am. My parents and I have different values."

"What does your father do?"

"He's a lawyer. He's a partner in a firm on Wall Street."

"My father owns a construction company," Ronan said. "We live near Sarah Lawrence."

"Well, now that we got that out of the way," Lyle said, "we can move on."

They did move on, and they became friends. They went to the coffee shop after the seminar and they talked for hours, mainly about the poems they were reading but also about their families and their classmates. They discovered that they had a lot of feelings in common.

Meanwhile, Ronan had found the complete poems of Hart Crane in the library and checked it out. He read the poems in chronological order, leading up to "Voyages."

Crane's images were striking and his use of words was original, and like most poets he was most effective when you read him aloud. His poems weren't easy to understand, but after reading several of them Ronan began to have a notion, and by the time he read "Voyages" he realized that it was about love.

"I knew you'd get it," Lyle said as they were having coffee after a seminar in which they discussed the assigned poems by Crane.

"It's a great poem. Why wasn't it assigned?"

"I told you. It was probably censored."

"But why would it have been censored?"

"That's a good question. You don't think it should have been censored?"

"No," Ronan said. "I don't see anything wrong with it."

"I don't either," Lyle said. "So we feel the same way about it."

The last week of classes, instead of going to the coffee shop after the seminar, they went to Lyle's apartment. It was on the fourth floor of an old building that had fire escapes, and as they climbed the stairs Ronan could smell exotic cooking.

"My neighbors are mostly Puerto Rican," Lyle explained.

The apartment was a studio with posters of Europe on the walls and books everywhere.

"You have a lot of books," Ronan said. Though he had always been at ease with Lyle, for some reason he felt a bit awkward in this situation.

"I love books. Would you like some wine?"

"Sure," he said as if he drank wine every day. In fact, his drinking experience was limited to an occasional beer with his father and his brother.

Lyle uncorked a bottle and poured some red wine into two juice glasses, saying: "I had wine glasses, but I broke them."

"That's okay."

He took a glass from Lyle, who went to a table and found a book.

They then sat down in the only chairs.

"Listen to this," Lyle said, finding a place in the book. He read in a voice he had never used in the seminar:

> All fragrance irrefragably, and claim
> Madly meeting logically in this hour
> And region that is ours to wreathe again
> Portending eyes and lips and making told
> The chancel port and portion of our June.

"That's great," Ronan said, feeling as if he had heard it for the first time.

"I never read anyone who wrote about love that way," Lyle said. "Did you?"

"No. I mean, not with the same wild abandon."

"You really get it." Lyle raised his glass in a toast. "To my friend Ronan, who understands what this poem is about."

Ronan reciprocated, saying: "To my friend Lyle."

They drank a toast to each other.

"You know, it's about us."

"What do you mean?"

"You know what I mean."

"I honestly don't know what you mean."

"I thought you understood that Crane was writing about his love for another guy."

"Another guy? No, I didn't understand that."

"I thought you did. You said you didn't see anything wrong with it."

"I said I didn't see anything wrong with the poem."

"Do you see anything wrong with a guy loving another guy?"

"I don't know. I never thought about it."

"Then think about it. How do you feel about me?"

"I like you," Ronan said without hesitation.

"I like you too. And when two people like each other, they should show it."

He saw where Lyle was going, and he remembered what had happened in Amy's basement. "I guess they should, but there are different ways of showing it."

"There are. But we should try what Crane was writing about."

"If it was with another guy, I can't imagine what it was."

"Yeah, you can," Lyle said gently.

"Well, maybe I can imagine it. But I can't do it."

"If you like me, you can."

"I do like you, but I can't do it."

"Then you don't like me," Lyle said, suddenly upset. From what he did next, Ronan learned what had happened to the wine glasses.

"I'm sorry," Ronan said, getting up from his chair.

"Go away," Lyle shrieked. "I never want to see you again."

On top of the building where Ronan lived was a water storage tank called a *tinaco*, but it had been empty since yesterday. The building had water since it was on the same line as the big houses on the ridge, but the water mostly remained in the cistern since they didn't have electricity to pump it up to the storage tank.

To flush their toilets and wash their dishes, Ronan and his neighbors hauled water from the cistern in buckets. Since it took two buckets to flush a toilet and Ronan was able to carry only one bucket at a time up the three flights of stairs to his apartment, he followed the usual water conservation policy: if it's yellow let it mellow, if it's brown flush it down. He ate his dinner off paper plates, reserving water for the pots and pans, and he didn't take showers.

Filo's center also had water since it was on the same line, but her *tinaco* was empty now and her inverter had run out of power, so her kids hauled water from the cistern in buckets. She offered to lend him a kid to haul water for his apartment, but he declined since he didn't want to have an advantage over his neighbors.

When he went to the clinic that afternoon he saw a water truck on the street with Daria standing by it. The truck was evidently filling her cistern.

"They'll sell it to me," Daria explained, "because I have a clinic. Right now it's the only water in the *barrio*."

Beyond the truck he saw women standing in line with buckets.

"It goes fast, so I'll have another truck here within a few hours. I hope they keep coming."

"Is there any news from the government?"

"No. Did you hear what happened in Santiago?"

"I heard from the guys at the round table. They don't miss a thing."

"If we didn't know before," Daria said, "we know now what the government cares about. It cares about the profits of foreign companies. It doesn't care about the people."

"I heard that a crowd marched on city hall."

"The people are angry. They're marching everywhere. We're going to march on the power plant. Would you like to join us?"

"Sure," he said. "When are you going?"

"As soon as this truck has emptied its tank. You can help me explain to our donors why we used their money to buy water."

"I think they'll understand."

When the truck was finished she paid the driver and asked him to come back with another tank of water. As an inducement she tipped him generously.

Then they joined a crowd of people who had gathered on the main street. There were men and women and children in school uniforms and babies in arms. Despite the lack of water, they were all wearing clothes that looked clean.

Among the people he noticed Padre Tavarez, and Daria headed toward him.

"Thanks for joining us, father," she said.

"I wouldn't miss it," he said with enthusiasm.

"Padre Tavarez, this is Ronan."

The priest shook his hand, saying: "I've seen you in church."

"I've enjoyed your homilies," Ronan said.

"Thank you. I don't often get compliments. Most people would be happy if I limited them to a few sound bites."

Daria led the procession with Padre Tavarez on her right and Ronan on her left. They marched through town and across a field on which a baseball diamond was laid out. On the other side of the field was a paved road that led to the power plant. They followed the road to a gate in the chain-link fence that surrounded the plant, and at that point a guy with a large pair of shears emerged from the crowd and approached the gate. He cut the padlock, removed it, and opened the gate, drawing a cheer.

They moved through the gate, heading toward the office. They were almost there when two *watchimen* with sawed-off shotguns took positions between them and the office.

Daria stopped about ten feet from the *watchimen*.

"Don't come any further," one of them warned her.

"If I do, will you shoot me?" she asked him.

"Our job is to protect the plant."

"We're not going to hurt it. We just want to talk with the person in charge."

"There's no one here."

"Someone's here. Someone's in charge."

"Well, we have instructions not to let you go any further."

"And we have a duty to talk with the person in charge."

Daria advanced, and the *watchimen* raised their guns.

"Remember the sixth commandment," the priest told them. "You don't want to put your souls in jeopardy."

"Then don't make us shoot you."

"We can't make you shoot us. You're responsible for your actions."

At that moment the door opened and a white guy appeared. Evidently the plant manager, he scowled at Daria and asked in English: "What do you want?"

"We want you to turn the power on."

"We can't. We don't have fuel to run the turbine."

"What about those tanks?" she asked, referring to the tank farm.

"They're all empty."

"I don't believe you."

"I don't care if you believe me."

"If you're telling the truth, you'll let me look into them."

"I can't let you do that," the plant manager said, evading her eyes. "It's against regulations."

"You have regulations, but you don't have principles."

"You got no call to say that," the plant manager growled. "We're only doing our job, ma'am."

"You're not doing your job. Your job is to generate power, and we haven't had power for almost three days."

"If the government paid us, we could buy fuel, and we could run the plant. But we can't run the plant without money."

"You have money. You have the money you gouged out of our poor country."

"This conversation isn't going anywhere."

"Young man," the priest said in English, "it's a sin to value money more than human life. And it's no excuse to say you're only doing your job."

"I haven't put anyone's life in danger," the plant manager said defensively.

"Yes, you have. You see all these people behind us? Without electricity they can't get water, and without water they can't live."

"They're still alive."

"They have health problems," Ronan said, "and you're making those problems worse."

The plant manager glared at him as if he was wondering what a fellow white guy was doing with this unruly brown mob. "If you want to be helpful, explain that we can't run the plant without fuel."

"I think you have fuel. I think you're playing a game with the government. You pretend you don't have fuel, you shut down the plant, and you hold these people hostage, hoping to get a ransom payment."

"You make us sound like drug lords."

"You *are* like them," Daria said. "You're doing what they do. You're willing to kill innocent people so you can make money."

"We haven't killed anyone."

"You're killing people every day with your poisonous smoke."

With a smirk the plant manager said: "We can't win with you. If we shut down the plant we're killing people, and if we run it we're killing people. What do you want?"

"I want you to stop killing people."

At that moment Ronan became aware of a car approaching behind them. It was the police car, and the crowd respectfully let it through.

"What the hell are you doing here?" Sergio asked Daria as he got out.

"We're trying to make this guy do the right thing."

"Maybe you are," Sergio said, "but you're breaking the law. You're trespassing on their property."

"They trespass on *our* property every day."

"They do? How?"

"By blowing their poisonous smoke through our streets."

"Well, they can't help where their smoke goes, but you can help where you go."

"They can filter the smoke so it doesn't pollute our *barrio.*"

"They have the technology and the money to do that," Padre Tavarez said, "but they don't want to spend the money."

"I understood that," the plant manager said in English. "The government inspects this plant, and it always certifies that we comply with regulations."

"What did he say?" Sergio asked Daria.

"He said the government always certifies that the plant complies with regulations."

"I believe it does. But I don't know what that means."

"You know what it means. It means they pay the inspectors."

Sergio sighed. "Well, that's outside my jurisdiction. Come on, Daria. Get your people out of here. I don't want to arrest you."

"What if I refuse to leave?"

"Then I'll have to do my job, but—" Sergio eyed the priest nervously. "If she won't leave, I hope you will, father."

"I won't abandon Daria," the priest told him, standing firm. "She's our extraordinary minister. Without her we can't do the Sunday mass."

Sergio turned to the plant manager. "Do you speak Spanish?"

"I try," the plant manager said in Spanish. "I studied it before I came here."

"When do you plan to turn on the power?"

"When the government pays us."

Sergio considered. "I have two uniformed officers, and you have two *watchimen*. There are about two hundred people here. If they came after you, we couldn't stop them. We could kill a few of them, but they'd overwhelm us and they'd kill you."

"Then call for reinforcements."

"My cell phone isn't working because there's no power to recharge it."

"You could use the phone in my office."

"If your phone's working, *you* could use it."

"What for?" the plant manager asked, looking puzzled.

"To call your boss and get his permission to turn on the power."

"Why should I do that?"

"If you don't, these people will come after you. And you know what?" Sergio said. "I don't get paid enough to risk my life trying to stop them."

"You could lose your job for doing this."

"Oh, I don't think so. I have two hundred witnesses who will say I did everything in my power to prevent violence."

The plant manager surveyed the crowd, which was becoming restive, and then he said: "All right. I'll call my boss."

"I'll make sure you do," Sergio said, following him into the office.

An hour later a cloud of steam blew from the plant with a deafening blast.

The people clapped their hands over their ears, and they looked afraid being so close to the plant, but they mostly looked happy.

Daria hugged Ronan and Padre Tavarez, saying: *"Gracias a Dios. Tenemos luz!"*

EIGHT

FOR THE MASS at eleven the next day the church was packed with people who evidently had come to give thanks for having electricity. Sitting in the back, Ronan recognized people from the march on the power plant that he hadn't seen in church before.

Padre Tavarez gave a special prayer of thanks, and he commended the people who had marched on the plant for their restrained behavior. He reminded them that the church opposed violence as a method for righting a wrong, implicitly condemning the method used by the Cobras, and he urged them to continue showing restraint in their protests against social injustice.

When the mass was ended Ronan waited for Daria outside the church, and they set off for the beach together, intending to have lunch at Joop's.

"I had the feeling," Daria said, "that Padre Tavarez was talking to me."

"Have you had any more conversations with him about blowing up the plant?"

"No. But he remembers the one we had."

"Well, he stood by you yesterday."

"He did. But that was nonviolent resistance."

"The church approves of nonviolent resistance?"

"It's what Jesus did. It's what Martin Luther King did."

"But it's only a step short of violence. His standing by you could have led to a battle between the crowd and the police."

"Like the one in Santiago," Daria said, stopping to let a car go by. "And I have to give credit to Sergio. He was the one who solved the problem."

"I don't know why, but I wasn't surprised by what he did."

125

"I haven't always had a smooth relationship with him, but after working with him I know that for him the most important thing is to keep the peace."

"So he's willing to compromise."

"He is. If you want to keep the peace you have to be willing to compromise."

After reflecting Ronan asked: "Are you willing to compromise on social justice to keep the peace?"

"That's a good question. For me the most important thing is social justice, so at times I'm not willing to compromise to keep the peace."

"Was yesterday one of those times?"

"Yeah, I was willing to go to war. And the only thing that stopped me was the thought of my neighbors getting hurt."

"Then if Sergio hadn't intervened, you wouldn't have let the crowd get out of control?"

"With the help of Padre Tavarez I wouldn't have," Daria said. "I asked him to join me for a reason. And he understood why I needed him there."

"You mean to help you control the crowd."

"That's right. And I think Sergio knew that with the priest there the crowd wouldn't get out of control."

"If Sergio knew that, then why did he intervene?"

"I think he sensed that the plant manager was afraid of the crowd, and he used that to make him do the right thing."

"So he was able to keep the peace *and* achieve social justice."

"Yeah. I guess that shows it's possible," Daria said. "But now that we have electricity again, the plant's polluting our air again, and we can't stop that by marching on the plant. It would take them at least a week to install filters, and we couldn't stand in front of their office all that time."

"Then you have to get the government to make them install filters," Ronan said.

"The government has no leverage over them. It owes them so much money."

"Would they ignore a government order?"

"They've ignored the law all along."

"Why doesn't the government enforce the law?"

"The government has no incentive to enforce the law. And it has a lot of incentive to allow them to ignore the law."

"Well, there must be a way to get the government to order them to install filters."

"There *is* a way. You could pay the officials more than the company pays them. But even that might not work because the company could ignore the order or shut down the plant until the government rescinded the order."

Ronan considered the situation. "That doesn't leave you many alternatives."

"It leaves me only one alternative, and Padre Tavarez never told me not to do it. He just asked how we could be absolutely sure that there would be no one inside the plant when we blew it up. And now I have an answer. I mean, I have a plan."

By now they were on the beach road, and two stray dogs had joined them, evidently having guessed that they were going to a restaurant.

"What's your plan?"

"As I told you, they have a night shift of two workers. They also have two *watchimen*. They order dinner every night from Solo Chivo, which a boy delivers on a motorbike. While he's getting the food, we disable his motorbike, and while he's dealing with the problem we put some knockout drops in the food."

"That sounds like it came from a pulp novel."

"It actually came from a television *novela*," Daria admitted. "So the workers and the *watchimen* eat the food and fall asleep, and we carry them out of the plant."

"How can you be sure there's no one left inside the plant?"

"We search the plant carefully. We look everywhere, and we make sure there's no one inside it. Then we put the explosives in key locations, and we withdraw to a safe distance."

"You need enough time to get away."

"We have enough time."

They passed a Haitian woman coming to the beach with a plastic basin of fruit on her head.

"And the plant blows up?"

"The plant blows up."

"Well, it sounds feasible," Ronan said. "But I have a question. What if the police catch you?"

"I'm willing to risk going to prison."

"But if you go to prison, then the people in the *barrio* won't have a doctor."

"I can be replaced."

"You can't be replaced. There's no one in the world who would care about the people in the *barrio* as much as you do."

"If that's true, then it's sad."

"It's a sad world," Ronan said.

For a while Daria was silent, gazing intently ahead, and then she said: "If they have clean air in the *barrio*, they won't need a doctor as much as they do now."

Joop got up from the round table and came over to greet them, giving Daria a kiss on each cheek and saying: "I have a table reserved for you."

"I didn't know you took reservations."

"I don't. But I can reserve tables for people I like."

He showed them to a table in the full shade, and they sat down, joined by the dogs.

Daria slipped off her shoes and buried her feet in the sand, closing her eyes and leaning her head back luxuriously.

Ronan was struck by her natural beauty, and for a moment he caught his breath.

"*Hola, doctora,*" Katiuska said, coming to their table.

"*Hola, Katiuska. Como estás?*"

"*Muy bien. Y usted?*"

"*Estoy muy feliz porque ya tenemos luz.*"

"*Gracias a Dios,*" the girl said with an upward glance.

"How did you cope with the outage?"

"We all helped each other."

"That's good. If we all help each other we can get through anything."

"*Profesor,* I like the two girls you brought to our home. We have a lot of fun together."

"I'm glad to hear that," Ronan said. "I know you're helping them to adjust."

"It's a very big adjustment," Katiuska said, speaking from experience. "It's like going from one world to another."

When the girl had left with their orders, Daria asked: "How do you like teaching there?"

"I like it a lot. I have two students, and both of them are eager to learn."

"If they were in New York, they'd be in seventh grade."

"In some respects they'd be way behind the other girls in seventh grade, and in other respects they'd be way ahead. It wouldn't be easy for them."

"In two or three years they'd be about where the other girls were in most respects."

"I guess they would be," Ronan said, unable to project their lives that far into the future.

"You know," Daria said, studying him closely, "you'd make a good father."

"Oh, I don't know. It's one thing to be a teacher, and it's another thing to be a father."

"You haven't talked much about *your* father."

"We don't have much of a relationship. I mean, he's a good man, but we never had any interests in common."

"Not even baseball?"

"That was our only interest in common," Ronan said. "We were Yankees fans."

"I was a Yankees fan, growing up in the Bronx."

"He took us to games, my brother and me. He had season tickets. He had a box."

"We sat in the bleachers."

"I'll bet you had more fun in the bleachers."

"You must have had fun," Daria said. "How could you not have fun at a Yankees game?"

"I did have fun when I was younger. But after a certain age I felt like I was a captive in that box. My father was always trying to get me to do what he wanted."

"What did he want?"

"He wanted me to major in business or engineering so that when I joined his business I could be useful to him."

"And you didn't want to join his business?"

"I didn't know what I wanted to do, but I knew what I didn't want to do."

"Did your brother join your father's business?"

"Yeah. And now they argue. My brother wants to do new things, and my father wants to keep doing the same old things."

After a silence Daria asked: "Is your father proud of your being a teacher?"

"I guess he is, but he never shows it."

"A lot of fathers have trouble showing their emotions."

"How do you know?"

"I see it at the clinic. In their rare appearances with their wives or children, the fathers don't show if they're worried or relieved. They just sit there impassively."

"My father isn't that bad, but there are emotions he has trouble showing."

"What about you?" Daria asked. "Are there emotions you have trouble showing?"

"Yeah, there are," he said, trying not to reveal how much the question rattled him.

"Is there one emotion in particular?"

He looked into her dark eyes and found something that gave him the courage to say: "I have trouble showing love."

"You do? Then what do you call helping me? What do you call helping Filo? And what do you call rescuing those girls from Arabian Nights?"

"I don't call it love."

"I call it love."

"I meant another kind of love."

"There's only one kind of love," Daria told him as if he was a child, "but there are many different ways of showing it."

"Well, maybe I have trouble showing love because I almost never felt it before."

"I assume you mean before now. So do you love Filo?"

"I do," he admitted. "I also love you."

She smiled happily. "You know, we talk about you. And we both thought you loved the other. So we were both wrong, and we were both right."

"But I don't know how to show my love."

"You're already showing it by helping us and standing by us. And since you didn't ask, I'll tell you, we both love you."

"Thanks," he said, feeling better about himself.

"Can I ask you something?" Daria said after a long silence.

"Yeah, go ahead," Ronan said uneasily.

"Have you ever had a girlfriend?"

"No. I never have." There was only one person he had loved before now. He felt an urge to tell Daria about it, but then he decided this wasn't the time, and he redirected the questions at her, asking: "Have you ever had a boyfriend?"

"No. I've been too busy. It takes time to have a boyfriend."

"The guys at the round table believe you're a virgin."

"I am a virgin," Daria said. "And I'll tell you why. I believe in the church's position on sex. I believe it's for union in love and for procreation."

"So you won't have sex unless you get married?"

"I won't have sex *until* I get married. I plan to get married and have children."

"Well, you won't have any problem finding a guy to marry you," Ronan told her.

"I may have a problem finding the right guy."

"I don't think you will. You only have to find a guy who shares your faith and your mission."

"Yeah, there must be a guy with those qualifications," she said, looking at him speculatively.

At that moment Filo arrived with her kids. They were all in bathing suits, and all but two of them raced to the water. Those two came over to the table with Filo.

"*Hola, professor,*" Lucy said.

"*Hola,*" Elvira said.

"*Hola, muchachas. Cómo estáis?*"

"*Muy bien,*" Lucy said. "*Tenemos nombres nuevos.*"

"*Me allegro.* Say it in English."

"We have new names."

"What's your name?"

"My name is Leticia. It means joy."

"It's a perfect name for you."

"My name is Elsa," Elvira said. "It means a promise of God."

"That's a perfect name for *you.*"

As the girls scampered happily toward the water Filo said: "They love you."

"I love them too," he said, conscious of what he and Daria had been talking about. With shame he remembered how he had been aroused by them, and he realized that if he had acted on his lust he would never have known love for them.

He glanced at Daria, who was smiling as if she could read his mind, and he smiled back.

"Guess what," Willem said, approaching the round table. It was the next morning, and the usual group of expatriates was sitting around, talking and drinking.

"The Cobras killed a policeman," Hans said.

Deflated, Willem stopped and stood there with his mouth open. "How did you guess?"

"It's a logical thing for them to do. The police killed a kid, so the Cobras had to get back at them and teach them a lesson."

"What was the lesson?" Donal asked.

"The sign on the body said: 'This is what happens to police who kill our children.'"

"Where did it happen?" Hans asked.

"I thought you knew everything," Willem said, sitting down.

"I can guess what they did, but I can't guess the details."

"It happened in Santiago, and they killed a member of the same unit that killed that boy."

"So they might not have killed the guy who did it."

"When police fire at a crowd," Donal said, "they never know who kills people. It's sort of like a firing squad with one blank round so that each of the guys who pulled his trigger can believe he didn't kill the person."

"Except that the police don't have a blank round," Hans pointed out.

"Where did they leave the body?" Ronan asked.

"In front of the police station," Willem said.

"They have *cojones*," Hans said.

"Or they paid someone off," Donal suggested.

"Oh, I don't believe that," Willem said. "I know you can pay any official to do anything, but you couldn't pay the police to let you kill one of their own."

"If he was already dead," Donal said, "they were only paying to dispose of the body."

"It would be like paying a funeral home," Hans said.

"I still don't believe it," Willem said.

"Then maybe they're just smarter than the police," Donal said. "I mean, they can get away with killing anyone they want."

"I wish I could," Hans muttered.

"Really?" Donal asked. "Who would you kill?"

Hans paused to think. "Well, it wouldn't be anyone around this table."

"I'm glad to hear that," Willem said.

"How many people would I get to kill?"

"I don't know. How many people have the Cobras killed?"

"Let's see," Willem said. "There was the reckless driver, the drug dealer, your countryman—"

"He wasn't my countryman," Hans said. "He was from Munich. They don't even speak our language there."

"Well, he was German. He wasn't Dutch. And there was the guy from the electric company, and now the policeman. That's five people the Cobras have killed."

"Is that all? It seems like they're killing someone every day."

"They're killing someone as often as they have a reason," Donal observed.

"Then I could kill five people?" Hans asked.

"That's your limit, at least for now."

Hans paused again to think. "You know, it's not as easy as you think. You feel like killing people all the time, but I don't know if I could do it."

"I thought you *had* killed someone."

"Where did you get that idea?"

Donal shrugged. "From people talking."

"Well, let me set the record straight. I never killed anyone."

"Then why are you here?"

"I want to be here. I could go back to Hamburg anytime I wanted. But why would I want to? Here I have everything a guy could dream of."

"I have a feeling," Donal said, "that you're not talking about the beer."

"I even prefer the beer here," Hans said. "But the women— There's no comparison."

"The women here," Willem said, "are the most beautiful women in the world."

"You're absolutely right," Donal said. "I've been everywhere, and I've never seen women as beautiful as the women here."

"They're not only beautiful," Hans said, "they're also generous and forgiving."

"Yeah, unlike the women back home," Willem said.

"You notice that Ronan isn't saying anything," Donal said, "because he has the prizes."

"Daria and Filo?" Willem said. "They're the most beautiful women here."

"So how did you get both of them?" Hans asked.

"I didn't get either of them in the sense that you mean," Ronan said. "They're my friends."

"Friends? It's not possible to be friends with a woman."

"Why not?" Donal asked as if he were playing the devil's advocate.

"If she's beautiful, you want to have sex with her. And if she lets you, then you're not friends anymore. If she doesn't, then why waste time with her?"

"You sound like you regard women as sex objects."

"All men regard women as sex objects."

"Ronan doesn't," Willem said.

"You don't know what goes on in Ronan's mind," Hans said.

"We just heard him say that Daria and Filo are his friends."

"I saw him with them yesterday," Donal said. "And I could tell how much they love him."

"They both love him," Willem said.

"That's an unstable situation," Hans said. "It's possible to have two women at the same time if they don't know about each other. But those two know about each other."

"They know I love both of them," Ronan said, hoping to end the conversation.

"How did we get on the subject of women?" Willem asked.

"We went from the Cobras," Hans said, "to killing people to why I'm here, and I'm here because of the women."

"Let's go back to the Cobras."

"They're your favorite subject."

"I'm interested in the Cobras because they're actually doing something. They're not just sitting around a table drinking and talking all day."

"Then why don't you join them?"

"I couldn't join them. I couldn't do the things they do."

"I could," Hans said, maintaining his position from an earlier conversation. "But I don't have their passion for social justice."

"I don't either," Donal admitted.

"I do," Ronan said. "But I reject their method."

"Their method works," Willem said.

"It only deals with the symptoms," Ronan said. "It doesn't solve the problems."

"Nothing will ever solve the problems," Hans said. "The world will always have rich people and poor people."

"The poor you will always have with you," Donal quoted biblically.

"So how would *you* solve the problems?" Willem asked.

"I don't know," Ronan said. "I guess I'd do what Daria and Filo are doing."

"At least they're helping," Hans allowed.

"All right, gentlemen," Donal said. "We have two competing approaches to the problems of the world. Should we place bets on which will prevail?"

"I don't bet," Willem said. "The last time I went to the casino I lost my shirt."

"You just don't want to bet against the Cobras."

"I'm not afraid of betting against them."

"I'm not either," Hans said. "I'm more afraid of betting against those two women."

They all laughed, including Ronan.

He was in his last semester at Fordham, and he still didn't know what he was going to do when he graduated. His father wanted him to get an MBA as his brother had, but he knew he didn't want to do that. He also knew he didn't want to keep living at home.

In early May he saw a notice on the bulletin board where they posted job opportunities. A missionary was looking for someone with experience in construction to join him in Colombia building schools. It sounded like a perfect job, so he wrote down the telephone number and called it from a public phone and made an appointment to meet with the missionary the next day in the college cafeteria.

If the guy hadn't been wearing a clerical collar, Ronan wouldn't have guessed that he was a priest. He could have been a member of the rugby team. But he had a magnetic force that attracted Ronan and made him feel that this guy was going to change his life.

"I'm Father O'Shea," the priest said, rising from the table and extending his hand.

"I'm Ronan. I'm glad to meet you, father."

"Please sit down. Would you like some coffee?"

"No, thanks. I'm fine."

"Well, let me explain what we do in Colombia," Father O'Shea said after a pause. "Our mission is to help people who live in the *barrios*. We organize churches and schools for them. We bring them hope. And we free them from oppression."

"Where in Colombia is your mission?" Ronan asked. In preparation for this interview he had studied a map and read the recent history of the country.

"Our base of operations is Popayán."

"Popayán?" He didn't remember seeing it on the map.

"It's a beautiful, old colonial city. But five years ago it had an earthquake that destroyed most of its churches and public buildings, not to mention thousands of homes. We went there right after the earthquake on a relief mission, and we've been there ever since. With funding from the World Bank, they've restored and rebuilt the areas that the tourists see, but there's still a lot that needs to be done, especially for the poor."

"You said in your notice that you were looking for someone with experience in construction. Do you actually build schools?"

"We actually build them, block by block."

"Well, I have experience in building offices and apartments."

"Where did you get this experience?"

"Working for my father during the summers."

"Did you like working for your father?"

"No. But I liked working."

Father O'Shea gave him an understanding smile. "I know what you mean. My father had a liquor store, and I worked for him during the summers."

"Well, I did learn a lot from him."

"I learned a lot from my father. How's your Spanish?"

"I studied it for four years. I was planning to be a teacher, and I thought that Spanish would be useful in the city schools."

"Are you still planning to be a teacher?"

"Yes, I am. But I want to do something else before I start teaching."

"It's good to have experience outside the schools before you start teaching."

"I thought it would make me a better teacher."

"It would. How long are you willing to stay in Colombia?"

"I don't know. I guess as long as I'm needed there."

"We're needed there indefinitely," Father O'Shea said, "but if you could give us three years of your life, we'd be very grateful."

"I could do that," Ronan said.

"Then you have a job. I've already asked about you, and they say you're a good student, a hard worker, and a self starter, which is more than I was at your age."

"When do we leave?"

"As soon as you're ready. I'll give you a list of things you should bring, and you'll need a few shots. Do you have a passport?"

"Yes. I do." He had gotten it for a family trip to Ireland, where his father still had relatives that he stayed in touch with. It hadn't been a fun trip since there was nothing for kids to do, and the adults just sat around and talked endlessly.

"Then you should be ready in about two weeks. If your parents have any questions, I'd be happy to meet with them."

"Thanks, father."

When Ronan got home he told Molly about the job. Her main concern was that he would be away for such a long time.

He told his father at the dinner table, and his father reacted as Ronan had expected.

"I don't want you to go to Colombia," his father said. "They're having a war there."

"They're having wars everywhere."

"And what the hell would you do there?"

"I told you. I'll build schools."

"You don't know anything about building schools."

"I know construction. I learned from the master."

"Don't get fresh with me, young man," his father said, looking at him sharply.

"I'm only saying I learned a lot from you, and that should make you happy."

"It does make me happy. But this idea of going to Colombia doesn't make me happy."

"It would give me experience."

"You can get the same experience here without the risks."

"You took risks. So why shouldn't I?"

"I did take risks. But I didn't go to a country where the most important business is drugs, where the government is fighting a war against communist guerrillas, where the murder rate is the highest in the world, where the—"

"All right, all right," Molly said. "We got the point. I thought the most important business in Colombia was coffee."

"It's not coffee. It's drugs."

"Well, we have a lot of drugs in our country."

"We get them from Colombia."

"The job isn't about drugs," Ronan said. "It's about helping people."

"You can help people here," his father said. "You can go and work in the South Bronx. They speak Spanish there too."

"But I want to have the experience of going to Colombia and working there."

His father sighed. "I can't stop you. But I can tell you what I've learned from life. Going to Colombia is a dead end. It won't help you in any career that I can think of, and it could get you killed in a stupid war."

"I think it would do a lot for me."

"Could we meet the priest you're going to work with?" Molly asked, mediating.

"Sure. He said he'd be happy to meet with you."

Father O'Shea came to their house the next evening and met with them. He made a good impression on them, and when he left they were convinced that Popayán was no more dangerous than the South Bronx.

Two days later when he turned the corner of the street where Filo had her center, he saw a police car parked in front of it.

Concerned, he rushed down the street and into the center where he saw Filo seated in a chair with a uniformed cop attending her. She was holding a bloody bandage to her forehead, and there was an ugly gash on her chin.

"What happened?" he asked.

"They sent goons to get Elsa and Leticia. We tried to stop them, but they had machetes, and they were bigger and stronger."

"They took the girls?"

"They took them back to Arabian Nights."

"Oh, God. I don't want to think about what will happen to them there."

"I don't have to think about it. I know what will happen."

At the moment he couldn't do anything for the girls, so he focused his attention on Filo.

"How did they hurt you?"

"They whacked me with a machete. They didn't want to kill me. They just wanted to leave a message. So they didn't use the sharp edge."

"I assume you're going to have a doctor look at those wounds."

"I'm going to the clinic as soon as Sergio is finished."

He put his hand on her shoulder, saying: "We're going to rescue Elsa and Leticia."

"We are," she agreed, covering his hand with hers and sealing their vow.

They were in that position when Sergio returned from the adjoining room, where he had evidently been questioning people.

Seeing Ronan, the detective said: "Wherever there's trouble, you're always on the spot."

"I'm not on the spot when it happens," Ronan said.

"I'm not either. I'm on the spot *after* it happens. And it's my job to find out what happened."

"Well, it's obvious what happened here. Those girls were kidnapped."

"They evidently were. But I don't know that. They could have gone willingly."

"If they'd gone willingly, then why did the people who took them away have to hurt Filo?"

"She tried to stop them. She might have become violent."

"I did become violent," Filo said, still holding the bandage to her forehead. "Those goons were kidnapping my children. I did what any mother would have done."

"You're not their mother."

"I'm their guardian."

"Not legally. And they don't need a guardian. According to their papers, they're eighteen."

"If they're eighteen, then I'm a hundred."

"Look," Sergio said, "I'm going to talk with them and get their story. If they tell me they didn't leave willingly, I'll bring them back. I promise you."

"They'll be afraid to tell the truth."

"I'll talk with them privately."

"That won't make them feel safe. After what happened, they won't feel safe until you shut that place down."

"If I find out they kidnapped those girls, I'll shut them down."

"Do you promise?" Filo asked, wiping away some blood from her eye and leaving him no wiggle room.

"I promise. Now, let's get you to the clinic."

Ronan went back later that afternoon to make sure that she was all right. He found her in the kitchen sitting on a stool, talking with the girls who were preparing dinner. She had pieces of gauze taped to her forehead and her chin. As she talked with the girls, gesticulating, he noticed that both her forearms were bruised, presumably from fending off blows.

"How are you doing?" he asked.

"I'm doing fine," she said. "But I'm worried. I haven't heard from Sergio."

"By now he's had enough time to talk with the girls."

"So why hasn't he brought them back?"

At that moment a girl came into the kitchen and said: "The

policeman is here. He wants to see you. I put him in the family room."

"Thanks, Olinda."

They found Sergio pacing the floor, looking agitated.

"Where are the girls?" Filo asked. "You promised to bring them back."

"I promised to bring them back," he said, "if they told me they didn't leave willingly."

"Well, they didn't leave willingly."

"They say they did. They say they don't want to come back."

"They're only saying that because they're terrified."

"They didn't look terrified."

"They've learned to hide their feelings."

"I'm sorry," Sergio said, "but if they want to stay there I can't make them leave."

Filo approached Sergio until her face was only a few inches away from his face. "So I guess I have no alternative but to *take* them back."

"I wouldn't advise trying that. If you do, they might use the sharp edge of the machete."

"Would you let those goons cut my head off?"

"I couldn't protect you in that situation. I couldn't give you a police escort to go and take back those girls."

"I didn't think you could. But don't worry. I don't need it."

Sergio stood there looking mortified. "What the hell do you expect me to do?"

"I expect you to protect those girls."

"But they don't want to be protected."

"They *do* want to be protected."

"Then why the hell don't they say what they want?"

"They're *children*," Filo said, raising her voice. "They're afraid to say what they want."

"My children aren't afraid to say what they want."

"Your children haven't been terrorized. Imagine them as slaves in Arabian Nights."

"I'd rather not," Sergio said. "I have enough to worry about."

"So you won't help me rescue them?"

"I can't help you rescue them. I don't have an army at my disposal."

"Well, thanks for your help," Filo said, dismissing him.

"I'm sorry," Sergio said, turning to go.

When he had left, Filo said: "At least he gave me an idea."

"He did?" Ronan said, wondering what it was.

"He said he doesn't have an army at his disposal, and we don't either. But we could get one. I know how to contact the Cobras."

"Oh, I don't think that's a good idea."

"I didn't say it was a good idea. But I don't have any other ideas. Do you?"

"No. But give me a chance to think of one."

"I'll give you until tomorrow morning. We can't leave Elsa and Leticia in that awful place."

"I know we can't," he agreed. "I made a vow, and I'm going to keep it. Don't worry."

She came to him and put her arms around him and pressed the unwounded side of her face against his neck and started weeping.

He knew what she was weeping for—not only for Elsa and Leticia but for all the children in the world who had been sex slaves, including herself. And Ronan felt as if her tears, which streamed liberally down his neck, could wash away the sin that had made him take a leave of absence.

NINE

As he walked on the beach the next morning Ronan considered Filo's idea of asking the Cobras to help them rescue the girls. She would insist that they avoid using violence, which they could do simply by using their reputation to terrorize the owners of Arabian Nights, but she couldn't be sure that no one would get hurt. And even if the Cobras pulled off the rescue without hurting anyone, associating with them could get Filo into trouble with the police, and if she was arrested, then what would happen to her center? What good would it do to rescue the girls if there was no safe haven for them?

Rejecting her idea, he tried to find an alternative. It didn't take him long to conclude that there wasn't anyone who could help them, so they had to rescue the girls themselves. By the time he reached the end of the beach he had an idea of how they could do it, and by the time he returned to Joop's he had a plan.

When he told Filo about his plan an hour later in the back office of her center, she said: "You could never get away with it."

"I think I could."

"If they caught you, they'd kill you."

"They didn't kill you."

"They would have killed me if I hadn't had witnesses. But you wouldn't have witnesses who were willing to talk."

"I'd have the girls."

"They'd be afraid to talk."

"They're afraid to talk on their own behalf, but if they saw another person get killed they wouldn't be afraid to talk."

"You could get them killed."

"Those people wouldn't destroy their valuable property."

Filo considered. "I really don't like the idea of asking the Cobras to help us, but I don't want you to risk your life."

"I already did that when I brought the girls here. Remember, those goons tried to kill me."

"But you might not be so lucky this time."

"I won't have to be lucky this time. I have a plan."

"Well, I think we should talk with Daria and see what she thinks."

"Okay," he said. "But I don't want the girls to spend another night there."

"I don't either. So let's see if Daria can meet us now."

Filo called Daria, who said she could meet them at Joop's in an hour.

Ronan and Filo were sitting at a table under a sea grape tree, with a stray dog napping at their feet, when Daria arrived on her motorbike.

"What's up?" Daria asked, wiping the dust off her face with the back of her hand.

"Sit down and we'll tell you," Filo said.

Daria sat down, giving the dog a pat on the head.

Before they could start, the girl who worked mornings came over and asked Daria if she would like something to drink.

"No, thanks. I'm fine," Daria said.

"Ronan has a plan to rescue the girls, and we'd like to know what you think about it."

"Okay. But I'm not an expert on rescue operations."

Ronan told her about his plan.

"If they caught you, they'd kill you," Daria said.

"That's what I said," Filo said. "But he thinks they might not kill him because the girls would be witnesses."

"The girls would be witnesses only if they saw them kill you."

"Well, I don't think they'll catch me," Ronan said.

"They'd spot you as soon as you came into the place," Daria said. "You've gone there before. They know who you are."

"I'm going to disguise myself."

"How?" Filo asked.

"I'm going to wear a hat and sunglasses."

"They'd see right through that," Daria said.

"You'd need a better disguise than that," Filo said.

"So give me some ideas," he told them.

"We could cut his hair short and bleach it blond," Filo said after checking him out.

"Yeah, we could make him look like a German."

"Except that he doesn't have a beer belly."

"We could stuff a pillow under his shirt."

"He'd have to wear shorts. They always wear shorts."

"Are you having fun?" Ronan asked, smiling.

"It's always fun to do a makeover," Daria told him.

"Could you really pretend to be a German?" Filo asked him.

"*Jawohl. Ich bin echt Deutsch.*"

"You sound just like one," Daria said. "Are you sure you're not part German?"

"I'm a hundred percent Irish. I studied German in college. So I'll finally have a chance to use it."

"Okay. You can speak German," Filo said. "But with your wavy reddish hair, you still look Irish."

"We can take him to Sylvia's to fix his hair," Daria said.

"And we can take him shopping to buy new clothes."

Then both the women turned serious.

"You really want to do this?" Daria asked.

"I don't see any alternative," Ronan said.

"We could ask the Cobras to help us," Filo said.

"If we did that," Daria said, "we'd be crossing a line."

"But we've tried everything. Aren't there times when violence is justified?"

"There are, and this may be one of those times. But the Cobras are terrorists, and if we used them for this purpose, what would that make us?"

"It would make us terrorists," Filo said glumly.

"And what if the Cobras killed someone while rescuing the girls?" Daria asked.

"It would make us killers."

"At the very least it would make us accessories before the fact. And we would have blood on our hands."

"So are we asking Ronan to risk his life so we won't have blood on our hands?"

"You're not asking me to risk my life," Ronan said. "I'm offering to risk it."

"But if they kill you," Filo said, "we'll be responsible."

"No, you won't be. You can't stop me from trying to rescue Elsa and Leticia. All you can do is help me reduce the risk of being caught."

There was a long silence, which Daria ended by taking out her cell phone. "I'll call Sylvia and make an appointment."

Father O'Shea lived in a *barrio* on the outskirts of Popayán. The *barrio* was hidden from the city by a thick barrier of willows, bamboo, and cypress trees. Between the *barrio* and the city was a field occupied by the decaying kiln of a brick factory, a prison compound, and the concrete pens of the municipal stockyards. A dirt road led into the *barrio*, which still showed effects of the earthquake. There were skittering chickens and sleeping dogs in the narrow dirt streets among the women balancing baskets on their heads and the men pushing carts. The houses were made of cinder block or panels of wood painted bright colors.

Father O'Shea's house was in the middle of the *barrio*. In front there was a large room that evidently served as a meeting place. Upon entering the first thing Ronan noticed was a quilt that covered a whole wall. In white letters on a blue background was the announcement: "The Lord sent me to bring glad tidings to the poor, to proclaim liberty to captives."

"A group of women made that for me," Father O'Shea said.

"It's the manifesto of liberation theology," Ronan said.

"Very good. Did you learn that at Fordham?"

"I remember it from a theology course."

"If the Pope saw that, he wouldn't be happy. He ordered us to distance ourselves from what he considers Marxist ideas."

"Is helping the poor a Marxist idea?"

"It actually came from Jesus, but it was adopted by Marxists."

"Well, you don't have to worry about the Pope coming here, do you?"

Father O'Shea laughed. "No. I only have to worry about the paramilitaries coming here."

Ronan had done research on Colombia, so he knew that the paramilitaries were unofficial groups that fought the guerrillas. "Why would they come here?"

"To look for guerrillas. They believe that since we and the guerrillas have the same goals, we must be working together. They don't understand, or they don't *want* to understand, that we don't use the same method. The irony is, the paramilitaries use the same method as the guerrillas, so at times it's hard to tell the difference."

"Are there guerrillas living in the *barrio*?"

"There are people who sympathize with them, but when you're hungry you don't have time or energy to get involved in politics."

Father O'Shea showed him to the room in back where he would live for the next three years, and then he took Ronan on a tour of the *barrio*.

As they walked around a puddle of water the priest said: "This is a *barrio de invasión,* which means that the people aren't from the city. They came from the country fleeing the guerrillas, the paramilitaries, the army, or all of the above. They were mostly farmers trying to grow enough to eat on small plots of land, and they were driven away by the war. In official jargon they're internally displaced persons."

"Do they have running water?"

"Some of them do, but most of them haul it in buckets from the springs."

"I noticed some women doing that. Are there sewers?"

"There are, but only about a quarter of the households have access to them. Many have latrines in their backyards. And some have no sanitary services."

"So what happens with their—waste?"

"It goes wherever. It breeds flies, and it spreads disease, and it kills children."

"Then maybe we should be building sewers," Ronan said.

"The problem isn't a lack of sewers, it's a lack of access to them. It's the same with food. The problem is a lack of access to it. That's the problem with everything. People don't have equal access to the necessities of life."

"What about schools?"

"There aren't enough schools."

"Are there enough teachers?"

"There are enough potential teachers. If we had schools, we could train teachers."

They stepped aside to let an old guy with a cart go by. The cart, which had a load of *yuca*, was drawn by a horse that looked as if it was on its last legs.

The first job, which they began the following morning, was to complete the expansion of a school in the *barrio*. They had three men from the *barrio* helping them, and Father O'Shea took off his shirt and labored with them, mixing cement and lifting it and pouring it into the molds for the columns that would support the roof.

As they were inserting rebar for a column Father O'Shea said: "This building is designed to withstand an earthquake of a far greater magnitude than the one we had."

"Did that earthquake destroy a lot of schools?"

"It destroyed more schools than it should have. The last thing we want is for a roof to collapse on a room full of children."

By lunchtime Father O'Shea had invited Ronan to drop the formalities and call him Pat.

When they returned to the house Pat insisted that Ronan take the first shower, a quick one since the water was limited and cold. They hung their sweaty work clothes on a line in back of the house, and they went into the kitchen where Pat began to make supper. Ronan knew nothing about cooking, but he could see that the quantity of food that Pat was preparing was more than enough for two people, and before it was ready he noticed that people had gathered in the front room and set up a table with folding chairs. When Pat and Ronan brought the food from the kitchen ten people—men, women, and children—were seated at the table.

"This is my family," Pat said. "It's different every night. They somehow arrange to take turns coming to supper."

Pat sat in the middle of the long table and asked Ronan to sit across from him. The people waited for Pat to say grace, and then they started passing the platters and bowls of food around the table. Clearly, the food was important to them, but as Ronan observed them he realized that their being with Father O'Shea was more important. While feeding them chicken and rice and beans, he was nourishing them with faith and hope and love.

Pat served as the parish priest in the local church, which he had rebuilt with the help of the community, and he offered a daily mass in the early morning, with two on Sunday. Though Ronan had attended church only intermittently while he was in college, he had no choice but to go to the daily mass and to both masses on Sunday. He had never been in church so much in his life. He found that a mass was a good way to begin the day, and he always learned something from Pat's homilies. Also, it helped him to improve his Spanish. Within a few weeks he could say all the responses in Spanish.

But what impressed him most was the evident faith of Pat's parishioners, who packed the church for the Sunday masses, not only the women and children but also the men. They performed the rituals with dignity, and except for the occasional crying baby they gave the mass their complete attention, bowing their heads and kneeling and rising in unison, with their eyes always returning to the crucifix above the altar.

At the end of the masses Pat always said a special prayer for peace, reminding them that a war was going on around them and asking God to protect them from harm. He invoked the patroness of the church, Our Lady of Peace, and he invited them to say a daily prayer to her for an end of the conflict that had ravaged the country for forty years.

It wasn't long before Ronan began to feel what the people of the *barrio* felt toward Pat, a love he had never felt before.

It took them a month to finish the project in the *barrio*, and then they went to a nearby village to build a school there. They drove to the village in a jeep that was older than Ronan but was kept in good working order by Pat, who seemed to know how to do everything.

One day, as they were taking a break for lunch, a pair of young guys with rifles slung over their shoulders came by and asked what they were doing.

"We're building a school," Pat told them.

"What are you going to teach there?" the shorter guy asked.

"Reading, writing, arithmetic. The basic skills."

"Are you with the government?" the taller guy asked.

"No," Pat said. "We're with the Catholic Church."

"The Catholic Church?" The shorter guy spat on the ground near Pat's feet. "So you're going to teach the children to be obedient servants of the rich?"

"That's not what we teach the children."

"It's what the church taught me."

"You don't look like an obedient servant of the rich."

The shorter guy smiled wryly. "I'm not. And you don't look like a priest."

"I am a priest. And like you, I want social justice. But I don't agree with your method."

"What do you know about our method?" the taller guy asked.

"You're carrying rifles, so you must use them."

"We do use them. We use them to kill capitalists."

"Well, you won't achieve your goal that way. You'll only make the government kill people."

"We don't make them kill people."

"You give them a reason to kill people."

"They don't need a reason to kill people."

"But if they didn't have a reason," Pat said, "they might not get away with it."

"They've always gotten away with it, and they always will—unless we change things."

"The way to change things is to change people, not to kill them."

"How is your school going to change people?"

"It's going to give them an opportunity."

"The rich will never give the poor an opportunity."

"The only way to give the poor an opportunity is to kill the rich," the shorter guy said.

"That's not the way," Pat said. "We could use some extra hands. Why don't you put down those rifles and help us build a school?"

"We don't want to build a school," the taller guy said.

"And we didn't give you permission to build a school here," the shorter guy said.

"You mean you issue the building permits?"

"We permit people to do what we want, and we don't permit people to do what we don't want. And maybe we don't want you to build a school."

"If you don't, then you don't want the poor to have an opportunity. You want them to remain poor so *you'll* have a reason to kill people."

"That's not true," the taller guy stammered.

"Then let us build the school," Pat told them.

The two young men withdrew for a consultation. It occurred to Ronan that their decision might be to kill these annoying gringos, but Pat didn't look concerned.

"All right," the shorter guy said upon returning. "You have our permission to build a school. But we don't want you to teach the children to be obedient servants of the rich."

"We won't. You have my word on that."

When the guerrillas had left, Ronan asked: "Did you know they weren't going to kill us?"

"Oh, yes. They're still young, they're still committed to their goal, and they know we're committed to the same goal. But if they'd been older, they might have seen us as a threat to their reason for being guerrillas."

"Then I hope we don't run into any old guerrillas."

"We probably won't," Pat said. "The old guerrillas aren't doing the dirty work. In that respect they're like our bishops."

Sylvia's beauty shop was on the main street across from Solo Chivo. In the shop there were three young women cutting or straightening or coloring hair, including Sylvia, who attended Ronan while Filo watched as if she was his mother.

"How do you want it?" Sylvia asked.

"Short," Ronan said. He didn't know the word in Spanish for a crew cut.

"Use the clipper," Filo said. "He wants to look like a German."

"Why does he want to look like a German?"

"To please me. I like Germans."

"Why do you like them?"

"I think they're sexy."

"But he's already sexy. And I don't think a short haircut will do anything for him. Why don't I just layer his hair?"

"He wants it short."

"All right," Sylvia said, reaching for the clipper.

Ronan looked in the mirror while Sylvia went over his head with the clipper, making his hair fall in bunches.

"How's that?" she asked Filo.

"He wants it shorter."

"It's a half inch."

"Well, make it three eighths of an inch."

Sylvia changed the attachment to the clipper and went over his head again.

"That's good," Filo said. "Now he wants it blond."

"Blond? Why blond?"

"To look like a German."

"But I love the reddish color of his hair. Why change it?"

"Just do what he wants. You know what they say— The customer is always right."

"But he didn't tell me to bleach his hair."

"I want you to bleach my hair," Ronan said.

"Are you sure?" Sylvia asked him.

"Yes. I want it *rubio*."

"All right," Sylvia said, looking for the bottle of bleach.

When she was done he almost didn't recognize himself in the mirror.

"That's perfect," Filo said.

"I think he looked better before," Sylvia said, shaking her head dolefully.

After they left the beauty shop Ronan and Filo got a taxi and went into Puerto Plata, where she took him to a department store. There they bought shorts with a tropical pattern and red socks to wear with his sandals. In a store near the central plaza they found a tee shirt with the Kaltenberg logo, and in another store they found the right size pillow.

He put the whole outfit together in the bathroom at Mike's Bar, and when he emerged Filo clapped her hands in approval.

"If I hadn't been with you," she told him, "I wouldn't recognize you."

"Well, let's see if it fools anyone," Ronan said.

Mike wasn't behind the bar, and Ronan hadn't ever seen the woman who was serving people, so there wasn't anyone to test his disguise.

They sat at the bar and waited for someone who knew Ronan.

Within a few minutes Mike returned and relieved the woman behind the bar. Mike greeted Filo and then asked: "Who's your friend?"

"Mein Name ist Fritz," Ronan said.

"Ein Vergnügen Sie zu treffen," Mike said.

For a moment Ronan was afraid that Mike would launch into a conversation in German, but then Mike said: "That's the only thing I know in German."

"I speak English," Ronan said with a thick German accent.

"Well, I don't have a Kaltenberg for you, but I can give you a Presidente."

"That's fine. It's very good beer."

"I'll have a white wine," Filo said, smiling.

They stayed at Mike's for a half hour and then after stopping at a bank to get the money he would need for the evening they took a taxi back to Santa Cruz.

The plan was for Ronan to go to Arabian Nights around seven that evening when it would be dark but still early. To kill time and avoid coming from his apartment he asked the taxi driver to leave him off at a bar on the beach road where clients of Arabian Nights were known to hang out. He hadn't ever been there, and he didn't expect to run into anyone he knew.

Before he got out of the taxi Filo leaned over and kissed him on the cheek, saying: "I'll pray that nothing happens to you."

"Thanks," he said, putting his hand on her forearm.

As the taxi drove away he walked into the bar, avoiding a dog that was asleep on the floor. The dog looked familiar, but it could have been any dog since they all looked alike. They were probably all related, descendents of the dogs that had come to the island with the Spaniards who had followed Columbus.

There were two big guys sitting at the bar that he didn't recognize. They were talking in German, so Ronan sat at the other end of the bar to avoid being drawn into a conversation. He ordered a Presidente, which he sipped slowly. He reviewed his plan, and when the time came to implement it he paid for his beer and left the place and headed for Arabian Nights, adjusting the pillow under his tee shirt.

The gate was open, and as Ronan walked through it he remembered the sight of the German hanging from the top with his mouth stuffed. If they caught him, they wouldn't hang him on the gate, they would throw him into the ocean. For a moment he wished he had gone along with Filo's idea of asking the Cobras to help them, but then he imagined all the things that could have gone wrong if they had done that, and he was recommitted to his plan.

The place was almost empty, so it had been a good decision to come early. He sat at a table from which he could see the whole courtyard, and he ordered a Brugal straight up. By the time the waitress brought it, the woman with the beady eyes and the parrot nose came over to his table. He remembered that her name was Vilma.

"Welcome to Arabian Nights," she said. "Is this your first time here?"

"*Ja,*" he said. "I have heard so many good things about it."

"Are you German?"

"*Ja. Ich bin echt Deutsch.*"

"We have a lot of German clients. Did you hear about us from one of them?"

"*Ja, ja.* Mine friend Helmut came here a month ago."

"Well, he must have had a good time."

"He had a great time," Ronan said. "He had two young girls together. He said their names were Lucy and Elvira."

Vilma appraised him. "They happen to be available, but you'd have to pay a premium to have them together."

"How much is the premium?"

"Twenty percent."

"So how much would be the total cost?"

"It's two hundred dollars for one of them, so two of them together would be four hundred plus the premium, so the total cost would be four hundred eighty dollars. You can have them for two hours. And you can do anything you want with them."

"I will pay you four hundred and fifty dollars."

"We have a deal. Pay me now, and I'll bring them to you."

Ronan reached into a pocket of his shorts and got out five one-hundred dollar bills and handed them to Vilma, who checked them with her beady eyes to make sure they weren't counterfeit. It occurred to Ronan that she could probably tell if they were.

"I owe you fifty," Vilma said as she left him to get the girls.

As he waited he worried that they would recognize him and give the game away, so he held his breath when Vilma brought them, handing him a fifty-dollar bill. He could tell from their eyes that they recognized him, but they were cool. Their faces had the hardened look of experienced professionals.

"Mine name is Fritz," he told them. "You are beautiful girls."

"Can we have the bridal suite?" Leticia asked Vilma.

"You can have it for two hours," Vilma said.

"Gracias," the girls said almost together.

He followed them into a colonnade that went around the main building. The bridal suite was at the end, and Leticia opened the door for him, standing aside with Elsa.

They went into the suite, and when the door was closed behind them Leticia said: *"Gracias a Dios.* That bitch didn't recognize you."

"I almost didn't," Elsa said. "You look like a German."

"I'm going to get you out of here," Ronan said. "But you have to help me."

"We can't go out the door," Leticia said. "A guard is watching."

"What about this window? Where does it go?"

"It goes out into the backyard, where they hang the laundry."

Ronan peered out the window into the dimly lit yard. "Is there a gate to the street?"

"No. But we could climb over the wall."

"Are you sure you can? That wall is higher than you are."

"If you help us, we can," Leticia said.

"If you help us," Elsa said, "we can do anything."

"Come here," he said, opening his arms to them. They were wearing short shorts and tops that exposed their belly buttons and their exaggerated cleavage. But they were kids, they were only kids, and his love for them was pure.

They came to him, and he hugged them, softly kissing the tops of their heads and saying: *"Que Dios te proteja."*

Quietly, they opened the window and one by one they climbed out. There were sheets hanging on the lines, which provided some cover for them. They moved through the sheets toward the wall, and then after making sure there was no *watchiman* in the yard, they went to the wall. Luckily there was no broken glass on top of it, as there often was on walls that surrounded houses of the rich.

"I'll give you a boost," Ronan said, making a stirrup with his hands.

"You go first," Leticia said to Elsa.

"What if there's someone on the other side?" Elsa asked.

"If there is, we're in trouble," Ronan said. "But there's no reason why there would be. If they're going to stop us, they'll do it on this side of the wall."

The girls nodded as if that made sense.

"Do you want me to go first?" Leticia asked.

"If it's all right with you, I do," Elsa said.

"Come on, come on. We're wasting time," Ronan said.

Leticia put a foot into his hands and holding on to the back of his neck she raised herself to a height where she could reach the top of the wall with her other hand.

She couldn't have weighed more than ninety pounds.

"Now, hold the wall with both hands," he told her, "and swing your legs over the top so that you can drop on the other side."

As she looked over the wall she said: "There's no one on the other side."

"That's good," he said. He watched as her hands let go.

She was smart enough not to call back to them and tell them she was all right.

"Okay. Your turn," he said to Elsa.

Encouraged by her friend's feat, Elsa followed her over the wall without any problem. The only difference from Ronan's perspective was that Elsa was even lighter.

Now it was his turn, and he had no one to boost him. But he could reach the top of the wall, and with all his strength he pulled himself up and got a leg over the top.

Before he swung the other leg over, he looked down and saw the anxious faces of the two girls, whose eyes were on him. It made him highly conscious of the fact that their lives depended on him, a position in which he had never been before.

He dropped to the ground, rolling to break the impact and quickly regaining his feet.

"Come on," he told them, taking their hands. "Let's get out of here."

They were in an empty lot with no cover, so Ronan led them along the wall away from the road and toward the back of a neighboring house. There was a wall around the house with broken glass on top of it, so they went around that wall to the next street, where Filo was waiting for them with a taxi.

When the girls saw her, they rushed into her arms.

"*Gracias a Dios*," she said, hugging them.

"Come on," Ronan said, opening a door of the taxi. "We don't want to stay here."

They all got into the taxi, which drove them to Filo's center.

The two *watchimen* they had hired in case the goons from Arabian Nights came after them were positioned in front of the center with sawed-off shotguns. At least for now it was the only way to make the girls feel safe there.

Instead of going for his usual walk on the beach the next morning, Ronan went to Filo's center and found the police car parked in front of it, as he expected.

Filo let him in and led him into the kitchen to give him some breakfast after explaining that Sergio was talking with the girls, getting their story.

Ronan was on his second coffee when Sergio came into the kitchen.

"Would you like some coffee?" Filo asked him.

"Yes, please. But I really need a shot of rum."

As Filo got up from the table, the detective sat down heavily.

"What did they say?" Ronan asked.

"They said they were kidnapped by goons," Sergio said. "They said they were taken away from here against their will and forced into prostitution."

"Did they have to work the night they were taken?" Filo asked with controlled fury.

"No. They didn't. But they were put into service last night."

"I can testify to that," Ronan said.

159

"They say you were their only client," Sergio said, "so there was no damage."

"You mean no further damage," Filo said.

"I mean no further damage."

In the silence that followed, Filo brought a mug of coffee to the table and set it down in front of the detective.

"So what are you going to do about it?" Ronan asked.

"I'm going to arrest the owners of that place," Sergio said with determination. "I'm going to charge them with kidnapping and using underage girls as prostitutes."

Filo, who was still standing, put her hand on Sergio's shoulder and said: "Thank you."

"Don't thank me. Thank the guy who rescued those girls."

"I already have," Filo said, looking at Ronan with bright blue eyes. "But maybe I haven't thanked him enough."

"You've thanked me enough," Ronan said. "And so have the girls. It was more than enough to see their faces when they realized I'd come to get them."

"I'm amazed that they recognized you," Sergio said, checking his appearance.

"They know him," Filo said.

"I don't know him. Who *are* you?"

"I'm a teacher on a leave of absence," Ronan said.

"Did you have a crisis in your career?"

"I did. How did you guess?"

"I'm having a crisis in my career."

"Then maybe you should take a leave of absence."

"Maybe I should," Sergio said. "But first I have to shut down Arabian Nights. And I'm going to take a lot of flak."

"I know," Filo said. "You said the owners have powerful friends. But those people might not come out into the open and try to stop you."

"Yeah, they might not want to admit that they're involved in prostitution."

"I'll be your witness," Ronan said. "I'll testify that those two girls were sold to me for four hundred and fifty dollars."

160

"And I'll testify that they were kidnapped," Filo said.

"Thanks," Sergio said. "But do me a favor. Don't do anything more about that place. You've done enough. Okay?"

"Okay," they said together.

Luckily, he didn't ask them not to do anything more about the power plant.

TEN

WHEN RONAN GOT to the clinic that afternoon Daria wasn't there. The girl at the reception desk said that the doctor was attending a patient at the hospital in Puerto Plata and that since she expected to be there for a while she had rescheduled her appointments.

He went into the back office and worked on a grant application. At one point his mind strayed and he imagined the scene at Arabian Nights when the police came to arrest people. The image of Vilma being taken away in handcuffs gave him particular satisfaction. He remembered the look in her beady eyes when she said: "I'll give you two for the price of one."

Ronan wondered what would happen to the owners. They might have to pay a fine, but they probably wouldn't do time in prison. They would pay off the right people, and they would lie low for a while, but then they would open another hotel for sex tourists somewhere else.

That last thought would have depressed him if he hadn't understood that Filo's mission wasn't to rid the world of sex slavery in one dramatic blow but to nurture a movement that would spread from town to town, from country to country, shutting down places like Arabian Nights one by one until the world was completely free of them.

He was checking the totals of projected expenses when the door opened. It was Daria, with a look on her face that he had never seen before, a volatile mix of sorrow and anger. She trudged into the room and closed the door and slumped into her usual chair, saying: "That's it. I can't let them keep killing people."

"What happened?"

"They killed another baby. She was eight months old, and her lungs were shot."

"I'm sorry," he said, feeling her anguish.

"I tried everything," Daria said with tears in her eyes, "but I couldn't save her. All I could do was call the priest and stand there while he prayed for her soul and watch her die. And she didn't die peacefully."

He knew there was nothing he could say.

"Those men in suits," she seethed, "those *white* men in suits who gouge money out of our country and poison our air should die the same way. If there were justice in the world, those men would choke to death on their money."

"God will judge them."

"I know He will, but I'm not going to wait for Him. I'm going to blow up that fucking plant."

He knew she meant it, but he was still conscious of the difference between wanting to do something like that and actually doing it. And he doubted whether blowing up the plant would solve the problem. "If you blow up the plant, they'll build another one."

"No, they won't. They won't be able to raise the money to build another plant."

"Then the shortage of power will be even worse."

"There are other ways to generate power," Daria said. "We have enough sun and wind in this country to generate all the power we need."

"But that would take money."

"We could get it from the World Bank."

"Then that would be the way to go. But before we blow up the plant, I think we should give the government one last chance to make the company install filters."

"They wouldn't take us seriously."

"Maybe they wouldn't. But they'd take the Cobras seriously."

"I thought we weren't going to ask them to help us."

"We don't have to ask them to help us. We could send a

163

message that looked like it was from the Cobras. We could set a deadline for making the company install filters."

Daria looked interested. "And what would the Cobras threaten to do if the government didn't meet the deadline?"

"They'd threaten to kill a politician."

"Why not threaten to kill the owner of the plant?"

"The owner of the plant isn't a person, it's a corporation."

"Then why not threaten to kill the governor?"

"It would tip their hand, and he would be heavily protected."

"So they'd threaten to kill any politician?"

"Yeah, the governor wouldn't know whom to protect. And there are so many politicians."

"Okay," Daria said. "I'm willing to try it. But the message has to look like it came from the Cobras."

"I can write the message. I took a course in calligraphy, so I can imitate the style they used for the sign they left on that German at Arabian Nights."

"You remember the sign?"

"I'll never forget it."

"Then write a message to the governor. Give him a deadline for making the company install filters, and if he doesn't meet it threaten to kill a politician."

After several drafts they had a message that said: "If you don't make the power plant install filters by September 10, 1999, then we'll kill a politician."

"That's good," Daria said.

"I could have been a Cobra."

"We all could have been Cobras."

He put the letter into an envelope, which he addressed to the governor, and then he asked: "How should we send it?"

"By regular mail."

"Is it reliable?"

"It is for letters to the governor."

"Well, I guess there isn't any other way. If we sent it FedEx, it could be traced. And if we had it delivered by hand, it could get the messenger into trouble."

"We can mail it at the post office in Puerto Plata."

"Do you want to sleep on this?"

"No, I want to do it now. Let's go." She got up and led him out of the clinic to her motorbike. He got on behind her, and as they lurched forward he held on to her.

Without really thinking about it he had joined her mission, and he was now committed to it.

On his way to the beach the next morning Ronan walked by Arabian Nights to see what was happening. The gate was closed and padlocked. A sign said: "*Cerrado.*"

Inside there was no activity. The fountain, the music, and the voices had stopped. Though the place had been closed only yesterday, with the litter of palm fronds on the pavement it already looked as if it had been closed for a long time.

Ronan took his usual walk on the beach, and then he joined the guys at the round table and ordered breakfast.

"That's what I heard," Willem was saying. "It's bad enough when an old person dies, but it breaks your heart when a baby dies."

"It's not the first baby in the *barrio* to die of lung disease," Hans said. "And it won't be the last. That smoke from the plant never stops."

"It stops when they shut the plant down," Donal said.

"They never should have put that plant there," Willem said.

"For them it was convenient," Hans said. "They got the land for nothing, and they have the use of a perfect port."

"There were people living on that land," Donal said.

"They didn't have titles for the plots they lived on," Hans said, "so they were easy to get rid of."

"They were moved into the *barrio*," Willem said. "And now they're being killed by the smoke."

"There are two things you don't want to be in these countries," Donal said sententiously. "You don't want to be poor, and you don't want to be in jail."

"How do you know?" Willem asked.

165

"I've been poor," Donal said.

"And I've been in jail," Hans said.

"Then you should feel for those people."

"I do," Donal said, "but not enough to get involved."

"I didn't come here to get involved," Hans said.

After a silence Willem said: "I wonder what the Cobras will do about it."

"About what?" Hans asked.

"About the baby. Will they kill the plant manager?"

"It's not the plant manager's fault."

"Then whose fault is it?" Willem asked.

"It's the governor's fault," Hans said. "He let them put that plant there, and he hasn't made them install filters. So the Cobras should kill the governor."

"But he wasn't governor," Donal pointed out, "when they put the plant there."

"Well, he's governor now," Hans said, "so he's responsible."

"If they kill the governor," Willem said, "it'll start a war."

"It won't start a war," Donal said. "It'll only start an election campaign."

"They must have a deputy who takes over if the governor dies or gets killed," Hans said.

"If there is a deputy, no one could tell you who he is."

"The deputy could. He knows who he is."

"If they killed the governor," Ronan said, "do you think it would change things?"

"What do you mean?" Donal asked.

"Do you think the next governor would finally make the plant install filters?"

"No," Hans said. "The next governor would take money from the power company, like the last governor and the one before and the one before. It'll never change."

"But everything changes sooner or later."

"That's not true," Donal said. "Most things don't change."

"Look at that stray dog that follows you around," Hans said, pointing to the dog that was lying at Ronan's feet. "Do you expect him to change?"

"We weren't talking about dogs."

"We were talking about politicians. They're the same."

"They're not the same," Donal said. "Dogs have integrity."

They all laughed, and the dog stirred as if he knew they were talking about him.

"They're going to kill the governor," Willem said.

"Well, you know how the Cobras think," Hans said, "so I won't bet against you."

"And it'll start a war."

"They won't kill the governor," Donal said.

"Then they'll kill a politician," Willem said. "They have to kill someone to avenge the death of that baby."

Ronan hoped that Willem was wrong about what the Cobras would do. If they killed a politician then the threat in the letter to the governor would have no value, and there would be no alternative to blowing up the plant.

The funeral for the baby was on Monday at eleven in the morning. Ronan sat in a back pew with Filo, who had left her kids at home. He recognized people from the *barrio*, but he hadn't seen the baby's mother before. She was sitting in the front pew with a woman who could have been her mother. There was no sign of the baby's father.

They stood as four boys carried the tiny casket up the aisle.

"Dales Señor, el eterno descanso, y que la luz perpetua los ilumine," Padre Tavarez said.

Ronan looked at the baby's mother, who had turned to watch the sad procession, and his heart went out to her.

He participated in the responses, but he had trouble paying attention to the readings. He kept thinking about the governor, who must have received the letter by now. Would he respond to it? Or would he simply hire guards to protect him from the Cobras.

He did listen to the homily, which Padre Tavarez began by saying: "Brothers and sisters, though we have come together in sadness we should not lose our faith, we should not lose our hope, and we should not lose our love of God and our love for each other. And we should not abandon our efforts to resolve problems peacefully."

Ronan looked toward Daria, but he couldn't see her face.

"We should do what this baby, who is now among the angels, wants us to do. We should use the power of God's love to convince people to do the right thing."

When the mass was ended they followed the casket out of the church and lingered among the people. In a few minutes Daria joined them.

"Where's the cemetery?" Ronan asked her.

"On the other side of town."

"Are you going there?"

"No. Only the family will go there with Padre Tavarez."

"I saw her mother and a woman who could have been her grandmother."

"That's the family."

"What about her father?"

"He didn't live with them, and I never saw him."

"Maybe he didn't know he had a daughter."

"Oh, he knew. They always know."

"And he never came around?"

"I didn't say he never came around. I said I never saw him."

"He should have come to the funeral."

"He couldn't have handled it," Daria said as if she knew. "And right now he's probably sitting on the Malecón with a bottle of rum."

"Are you going back to work?" Filo asked.

"I don't know. I don't feel like it. But I guess I should."

"You should take a break."

"I should join the father with his bottle of rum."

"Come on," Filo said, taking her arm.

They went to the café next to the beauty shop and sat at a table out of the way.

When they had ordered coffee Daria said: "When Padre Tavarez talked about not abandoning our efforts to resolve problems peacefully, did you think he was talking to us?"

"Yeah, I thought he was," Ronan said. "But we're still trying to resolve the problem peacefully."

"What if the governor doesn't meet our deadline?"

"We're not going to kill a politician."

"No. We're going to blow up the plant."

"Then we should work out the final details of our plan."

"I know how we're going to get the people out of the plant," Daria said. "But how are we going to get the explosives?"

"We can get them from a supplier of construction materials," Ronan said.

"You mean you can just buy them?"

"You can in my country if you're a licensed construction company."

"What do construction companies use explosives for?"

"For blasting rocks at construction sites."

"Then we need to find a licensed construction company that will work with us."

"No, we don't. We can pay off the supplier."

"Who would deal with the supplier?" Filo asked.

"I would," Ronan said.

"Then you'd have to use a disguise again, and maybe this time you should be an American."

"Yeah, that would be in character. We're always paying off people to do illegal things."

"Well, I hope we get a positive response from the governor," Daria said. "I really don't want to blow up the plant."

On Sunday evenings after cleaning up the kitchen, Pat would share with Ronan his only indulgence, a bottle of *aguardiente* called Blanco del Valle. They would have a shot or two of the liquor, which they sipped slowly while they talked about a wide range of subjects, including their work and the people in the *barrio*. Sometimes Pat would talk about people he had known elsewhere, or people who had influenced him. One evening he talked about a priest in Argentina, who had been his role model.

"His name was Carlos Mugica," Pat said, gazing across the candlelit room. "He came from a prominent family, and with his connections he could have done anything he wanted. But he decided to become a priest and serve the people. His family got him assigned to a church in Barrio Norte, a wealthy neighborhood of Buenos Aires, which wasn't what he had in mind, and he promptly got himself unassigned by telling the rich parishioners that they had a responsibility to help the poor. The archbishop tried to talk him into leaving the priesthood, but he resisted, and he went to a *barrio* like this one—in Buenos Aires they're called *villas miseria*—and got himself assigned to a church called Christ the Worker."

"How did his family react to that?"

"They weren't happy. It sounded Marxist, and at that time in Argentina there was a conflict between the left and the right that ultimately led to civil war. On the left were the Montoneros, who evolved from a group of Catholic activist students, and on the right were the fascists. It was similar to the situation we have here, except that in Argentina the military took over the government and pursued a total war against the leftists. But that didn't happen until later," Pat said. "In the meantime Carlos got involved in liberation theology and the movement of priests for the third world, and he advised the Montoneros. So he was on the right wing's shit list."

"What period of time was that?"

"From the late sixties to the early seventies."

"Did you ever meet him?"

"Yes. I was in Argentina in the early seventies. I was a lay worker in a *villa miseria*. When I heard about Carlos, I went to the *villa* where he worked. I saw as much of him as I could, and I learned a lot from him, not only by talking with him but also by reading things he wrote. In addition to being a man of action, Carlos was a man of thought. I have some of his writings, which you can read if you'd like to."

"I would," Ronan said, wanting learn more about this man.

"What impressed me most about his writings was his emphasis on love. Of course love is central to our religion, and we all talk about it, but we don't always practice it, especially when we encounter people who arouse the opposite feeling. And even with people who don't arouse the opposite feeling, we often withhold our love from them because we don't want to let go of ourselves, or because we're afraid to let go of ourselves. For whatever reason we hold back, we refuse to love, and that has serious consequences."

"What kind of consequences?"

"It hurts other people, and it hurts us. Carlos put it in a nutshell when he said: '*Pecar es negarse a amar.*' "

"Sin is refusing to love?"

"That's a good translation. We refuse to love when we think only about ourselves. Carlos called it the sin of egotism. We sin when we treat another person like a thing. And that, he said, is the ultimate sin—the sin against love."

"But how do we avoid committing that sin?"

"By not thinking about ourselves. By thinking and caring about other people." Pat paused, and then he added: "Of course it's not easy. We have to work at it."

"How do we work at it?"

"By doing things for other people."

"What kind of things?"

"Little things, everyday things."

"You mean like cooking dinner for them?"

"Yeah," Pat said. "And listening to them, paying attention to them, caring about them, hoping for them, and praying for them. I learned that from Carlos."

"What happened to him?"

Pat took a slow sip of *aguardiente*. "Even before the military took over, the right wing members of the party in power, the *peronistas*, started eliminating people who they thought had Marxist tendencies. One evening, as Carlos was leaving church after celebrating mass, he was killed by an assassin who riddled him with bullets."

"Oh, my God," Ronan said. "They murdered him in cold blood?"

"In the war that followed, they murdered thousands of people in cold blood. They kidnapped them, they tortured them, and they made them disappear."

"Did they bother you?"

"They arrested me, and I thought they were going to kill me, but for some reason they let me go, and they escorted me out of the country."

"Where did you go?"

"I went back to New York. And I enrolled in the seminary."

"You wanted to carry on his mission."

"That's right. His mission of love."

One Sunday evening they were talking and sipping *aguardiente* when a young woman appeared in the doorway with a look of desperation in her dark eyes.

"I'm sorry to bother you, father," she said humbly.

"It's all right," Pat said, putting down his shot glass. "What can I do for you?"

"I'm from a village where you built a school. Do you remember me?"

"Oh, yes," Pat said. "Your husband worked with us."

"That's right. He still talks about you."

"God bless him. But you didn't come here to talk about your husband. What happened?"

"Some men came to our village," the woman said. "They said we were feeding the guerrillas. And they killed three people, including the oldest son of my sister."

"I'm so sorry," Pat said. He went to the woman and put his arms around her and held her.

The woman cried for a while in his arms, and then she said: "We want the boy to have a proper funeral, but the local priest is afraid of those men, so he won't do anything in public. He'll only say a prayer for the dead."

"When was the boy killed?"

"He was killed yesterday."

"You can spend the night here," Pat said, "and I'll go with you tomorrow morning."

"Thank you, father," the woman said.

Ronan intended to go with them, but before they left the next morning Pat asked: "Are you sure you want to go with me?"

"Yes. I'm sure."

"It's dangerous."

"I know. Wherever you go, I want to go with you."

Pat laid a hand on his shoulder, saying: "May God bless you, and may God protect you."

They took the jeep with the woman in front and Ronan in back, following a dirt road to the village.

It was the village where the two guerrillas had accosted them. Except for the usual stray dogs the streets were empty, giving the impression that the inhabitants had been driven away and become internally displaced persons.

When they stopped at the house of the woman's sister people started appearing, and the word evidently spread around that the priest from Popayán was there. They formed a procession and carried the boy's coffin to the church, defying the men who had killed him.

The local priest was standing in the door as if he was going to stop them, but the look on his fearful face changed when Pat said: "The Lord be with you."

"And also with you," the local priest responded.

Pat performed the funeral with the local priest assisting, and there was no trouble until they left the church following the casket.

Outside, a band of men with rifles was waiting for them.

"Who are you?" a guy with a black mustache, evidently the leader, asked Pat.

"*Soy cura,*" Pat said. "I am a priest."

"I can see that, but where did you come from?"

"I came from Popayán."

"I mean before. You look like a gringo."

"I'm an American."

"What are you doing here?"

"I'm performing a funeral for a boy who was killed for no reason," Pat said.

"He was killed for a reason. He was a guerrilla."

"They say he wasn't a guerrilla."

"Well, they're lying. They're covering up for him."

"Whatever he was, it was wrong to kill him."

"It's not wrong to kill guerrillas," the leader argued "They're raping our women, they're kidnapping our men, and they're killing our children."

"You're doing the same thing to them."

"We're only acting in self-defense."

"This boy wasn't killed in self-defense. He was killed in cold blood."

"If that's what these people say, they're lying. He attacked us."

"He didn't attack you," the mother said. "He was in our home. You dragged him out into the street and shot him."

"That's the wonderful thing about mothers," the leader said. "No matter what their children do, they always stick up for them."

"I'm not his mother," another woman said. "I saw what you did. I saw you kill him."

"Well, it looks like you people didn't learn your lesson," the leader said, beginning to take his rifle off his shoulder.

"Stop," Pat told him quietly.

"Stay out of it," the leader warned him.

"I'm not going to stay out of it. In the name of the Lord, I'm telling you to stop. I'm telling you to go away and let us bury this innocent boy."

"What if I don't do what you say?"

"You'll have to deal with God," Pat said unflinchingly.

"All right, all right. You can bury that bastard. But I don't want to see you here again."

"If you kill any more people, you'll see me."

"Not if I kill you," the leader said, tightening his grip on the strap of his rifle.

"I won't try to have the last word," Pat said, beginning to move toward the casket. "God will have it."

As the week passed and there was no response from the governor they prepared to implement Daria's plan by having dinner more than once at Solo Chivo at the time when the plant ordered food for the night-shift workers and the *watchimen*. They saw where the boy parked his motorcycle while waiting for the food to be ready, and they noticed how his mind was focused on a pretty waitress who flirted with him. That would give them an opportunity to disable his motorbike, and depending on where he left the food while he was dealing with the problem, they would somehow gain access to it.

In the meantime they had an opportunity to talk with the governor, which arose thanks to one of Daria's local donors. On Saturday, September 4 the governor was holding a concert at his home for the benefit of the national symphony orchestra. The main attraction was a Dominican tenor who performed with major opera companies around the world, including the New York City Opera.

Tickets to the event had been made available to the *gente bien*, as Daria called them, and one of her donors had three tickets available, free of charge, so they decided to take advantage of the unexpected opportunity.

For this occasion the two women had their hair done at Sylvia's, and they wore pantsuits, Daria in black and Filo in white. On another trip to the department store in Puerto Plata, Ronan found a pair of khaki slacks and a light blue *chacabana* that would be suitable. By now his hair had two layers of color, so he went to Sylvia's and had his head completely shaved.

"You look like an Irish monk now," Daria told him.

"There's an idea for a new career," Ronan said, smiling.

"Oh, I can't see you as a monk."

"What can you see me as?"

"I guess I can see you as a Cobra."

"Do they have shaved heads?"

"I don't know. I've never seen a Cobra."

At three in the afternoon on Saturday they took a taxi to the governor's house, which was in an area of Puerto Plata where the old rich families still had houses. It was a large Spanish-style house with an ample lawn on which rows of folding chairs had been set up, facing a stage.

Within a few minutes of their arrival a waiter stopped to serve them champagne.

After taking a tentative sip Filo said: "This is okay, but I prefer Presidente."

"Imagine living like this," Daria said, looking around.

Ronan didn't have to imagine since he had grown up living like this.

"Oh, there's the governor," Filo said, nodding her head at a tall guy who stood nearby.

"Let's go and talk with him," Daria said.

They approached the governor as he was about to move on.

"Ladies," he said, inclining his head toward Daria and Filo. He was an attractive guy, with a pleasing smile and expensive-looking clothes. He looked pure white.

"I'm Daria Sanchez," Daria said, extending her hand.

The governor graciously took it, saying: "Are you the famous Dr. Sanchez?"

"I'm not famous, but I'm a doctor. And this is Filomena Romero. She runs a center to rescue girls from sex slavery."

"*Un placer.* And who are you?" the governor asked, looking at Ronan curiously.

"I'm Ronan Byrne. I work for them."

"You're lucky to work for two such beautiful ladies."

"We lost another baby in the *barrio* of Santa Cruz," Daria told the governor.

"I'm so sorry. What did the poor thing die of?"

"She died of lung disease, caused by the smoke from the power plant."

"It couldn't have been that," the governor said, shaking his head. "The smoke from that plant is filtered. It's perfectly safe."

"We have data that show it's loaded with toxins."

"You must be mistaken. I saw data that show it's safe."

"You saw data they wanted you to see. They probably got it from a plant in America."

"They say they got it from this plant."

"They're lying."

"Well, I don't know why they would lie."

"I do," Daria said. "They'd lie because they don't want to spend money on filters."

"They showed me evidence that they installed filters."

"Again, they probably showed you evidence from a plant in America."

"I don't believe you," the governor said. "The people who operate that plant are honorable."

"They're not honorable," Daria said. "They're only interested in making money."

"I have the impression that you don't like them."

"I don't like people who kill for money."

"Excuse me," the governor said. "It's been a pleasure talking with you, but I have to go and talk with my other guests."

When he had left them Filo said: "I don't think he was listening to you."

"They never listen. They just talk."

"Well, you tried."

"I tried."

At that moment the buzz of conversation was interrupted by the sound of a whistle like one used by a sports referee.

"Don't anyone move," a voice from a megaphone ordered them.

Looking toward the voice, Ronan saw the governor with his hands up and a guy pointing a pistol at him. Then out of nowhere two more guys were standing in front of Daria, Filo, and him, pointing pistols at them.

"Raise your hands," one guy said.

The other guy searched them. When he had patted them all down and confiscated Daria's cell phone, he said: "They're not armed."

"Now, put your hands behind you."

They did, and they were quickly handcuffed.

"Do what we say," the guy who was giving them orders said, "and you won't get hurt. Now, come with us."

The guys herded them across the lawn and out the gate, behind the governor. Two jeeps were waiting for them, and the apparent leader ordered them to get into the jeeps, the governor and Filo in one, and Ronan and Daria in the other.

Then the jeeps lurched forward and took them away.

ELEVEN

THE JEEPS HEADED west toward Santa Cruz as fast as the traffic allowed. As they passed the *teleférico* Ronan looked up at the mountain and saw a dark cloud that was hiding the statue of Christ the Redeemer.

The two guys in front of the jeep hadn't exchanged a word since they left the governor's house, giving no hint of who they were or where they were going or why they had taken hostages. He assumed they were the Cobras, though this wasn't like any of their previous operations. Their normal pattern was to kill people, not to take hostages.

He glanced at Daria, whose brow was furrowed as if she was trying to figure out what was happening. When their eyes met, her expression said: "I have no idea."

Wherever they were going, it was a place where the police couldn't find them. And from there the Cobras would make some demand. Did they want money to finance their operations? Did they want to change the government?

They passed the main road that went into Santa Cruz and continued going west until they came to another town, and then they headed south toward the mountains. For a while they were on a paved road, and then they turned onto a dirt road, which rose steeply. After climbing for a while the road leveled off and become only a two-track trail. They crossed a stream in which the water came up almost to the floor of the jeep, and then they bumped along for a while until they crossed what could have been the same stream winding through the valley. Then they climbed again, slowly.

Ronan couldn't see his watch but he figured it had been about an hour since they left the governor's house, and it had been

179

about a half hour since they left the paved road. They had probably averaged about ten miles per hour since then, so they were probably about thirty miles west of Puerto Plata and about five miles inland from the coast.

Ahead he saw a sign at the edge of the trail that said: "Rancho Escondido." They were now on a gravel driveway that led to the entrance of a building. They stopped under a rustic carport, allowing enough space for the jeep behind them.

The driver jumped out, leaving the keys in the ignition, probably so they could make a quick getaway if necessary.

"Get out," the guy in the passenger seat told them.

Ronan was stiff, and since he was unable to use his hands to steady himself, he was wobbly getting up. The guy who had ordered them to get out helped him.

"Thanks," Ronan said.

The guy said nothing, evidently limiting to the necessary minimum his interactions with a person he might have to kill.

They walked along a covered path to the entrance of the place, which looked as if it hadn't been occupied for years. It must have been a resort for people who wanted to spend a vacation in the mountains. Inside was a sitting room with cushioned armchairs and a coffee table on which there were a few old magazines.

"Sit down," the guy said.

Ronan and Daria sat down. They didn't lean back because of the handcuffs. They waited in silence until Filo and the governor were led in and told to sit down.

By then all four guys were in the room, and one of them took charge. He was tall and lean, about thirty, with a grim mouth and intense eyes. In a slow, deliberate voice he said: "We'll begin by introducing ourselves. My name is Ernesto."

Ernesto paused and let the other three guys introduce themselves.

Ronan doubted that they were using their real names.

"I know who *you* are," Ernesto said, glaring at the governor, "but I don't know who the rest of you are. Please introduce yourselves."

"My name is Daria. I'm a doctor."

"My name is Filomena. I'm a social worker."

"My name is Ronan. I'm a teacher."

"You're not from here," Ernesto said.

"No, I'm from New York."

"Where in New York?"

"Yonkers," Ronan said.

"I know where that is. I lived in the Bronx when I was a kid. Are you on vacation here?"

"No, I'm on a leave of absence."

"Now that we all know each other," Ernesto continued, "I'll explain why we brought you here. We're holding you as hostages, and we're going to make a demand of the government. If it does what we ask, we'll let you go unharmed. If it doesn't, we'll kill you. *Entienden?*"

They nodded.

"And if you try to escape, we'll kill you. *Entienden?*"

They nodded again.

After a silence Daria said: "Could you tell us what you're asking the government to do?"

"You don't need to know that," Ernesto said.

"We don't, but I think we're entitled to know it. Our lives are at stake."

Ernesto looked at Daria as if he was seeing her for the first time. "What kind of doctor are you?"

"I'm a family practitioner with a specialty in pulmonology."

"Pulmonology? Then you know what that power plant is doing to our children."

"I see what it's doing every day. I run a clinic in the *barrio* of Santa Cruz."

"Then you should support what we're asking the government to do."

"Are you asking them to make the plant install filters?"

Ernesto laughed bitterly. "The filters are a joke. They claim they already installed them. But they're lying."

"I know they're lying," Daria said, glancing at the governor.

He stared at the floor evasively.

"We're asking the government," Ernesto said, "to make the company tow the plant out to sea and sink it."

"You mean blow it up?"

"Yeah, blow it up and sink it. So they can't take it to another poor country."

"I support your goal," Daria said. "But I don't support your method."

"In your position you wouldn't," Ernesto said, "but in my position you would."

"I wouldn't support your method in any position. It's morally wrong. It goes against the teachings of our church."

"Oh, I should have noticed the crosses," Ernesto said, looking from Daria to Filo and then asking Ronan: "Where's your cross?"

"On top of the mountain," Ronan said.

Ernesto laughed. "That's one thing I like about Americans. Even when they're in a bad position they still have a sense of humor."

"I was being serious. And your cross is up there too."

"I don't have a cross. I don't care about religion."

"What do you care about?"

"Social justice."

"Do you care about your family?" Filo asked.

"I don't have a family."

"You don't have a mother, a father, a sister, or a brother?"

"No. I don't have anyone."

"I don't either. But I care about people."

"I care about people," Ernesto said. "That's why I want social justice."

"We all want social justice," Daria said. "Don't we, governor?"

The governor nodded weakly, looking as if he was about to pee in his pants.

"You might be wondering," Ernesto said, "why we didn't just take the governor. We need extra people we can kill to show we're serious. We'll give them a deadline, and if they don't act by then we'll start killing you."

"What's the deadline?" Ronan asked.

"You think you're entitled to know that too?"

"Yeah, I think we are. How long will you give the government before you start killing us?"

"We'll give them until Wednesday. If we don't see any action by then, we'll kill one of you. And you'll decide which one it is."

"You mean other than the governor."

"We wouldn't kill the governor first. If we did, then we wouldn't have any more leverage. They don't care about the rest of you."

"So you didn't select us for any reason."

"That's right. We could have taken anyone with him, but you were there together, and we wanted two women."

"Why did you want two women?" Daria asked.

"If we kill a woman, we'll get more attention. It's ironic because men mostly treat women like shit. They beat them, they abuse them, and they kill them. And people just take it for granted. But if *we* kill a woman, then the men who beat them, abuse them, and kill them will be outraged. I wonder why."

"It gives those men," Filo said, "a chance to pretend they would never hurt a woman."

"Well, I'd rather not give them that chance," Ernesto said. "But I will if I have to."

"I need to go to the bathroom," the governor complained.

"We'll show you the way, and we'll show you to your rooms."

They were put in separate rooms so they couldn't talk with each other. Ronan's handcuffs were removed for the night, but his door was locked from the outside and his window was barred. The wrought-iron grill prevented thieves from breaking in but it also prevented hostages from escaping. The window offered a view of the mountain, and in the moonlight Ronan could see the back of Christ the Redeemer.

He didn't sleep much, and when it was finally light he heard the sound of a helicopter overhead. It was evidently part of a search mission, but it didn't raise his hopes since he assumed that from the air they wouldn't see the jeeps under the carport, and they wouldn't see any other evidence that people were staying at Rancho Escondido.

A few minutes later a guard unlocked his door and let him out to go to the bathroom and have breakfast. The guard escorted him to the kitchen, where Daria and Filo were sitting at a table, eating *mangú*, a Dominican dish of mashed green plantains.

"I hope you like *mangú*," Daria told him. "We're probably going to have it every day."

"At least until Wednesday," Filo said, dipping her spoon into her bowl.

Ronan helped himself from the pot on the stove and sat down with them, conscious of the two guards watching them. For a while he hesitated to talk, but then he realized that it didn't make any difference what the guards heard them say as long as they weren't plotting to escape. So after tasting the *mangú* he said: "I wonder how they're going to deliver their demand."

"They must have someone in place to do that," Daria said.

"They haven't taken a jeep anywhere," Filo said.

"So how will they know if the government has done what they want?"

"They must have signals," Daria said. "They have a view of the mountain from here."

"I saw it last night," Filo said. "The mountain was beautiful in the moonlight."

"I saw it too," Ronan said. "I had the feeling that Christ had turned his back on me."

"I didn't have that feeling. I had the feeling that He was leading me."

"Leading you where? You were locked in your room."

"My body was, but my soul was free."

They were silent in respect for this statement.

Then Daria said: "I'm wondering about these guys. They're not at all what I expected."

"What did you expect?" Ronan asked after swallowing a mouthful of *mangú*.

"I expected guys acting on impulse. But they must have planned this operation."

"Yeah, they must have."

"And it's not the usual pattern of the Cobras. They usually respond to the death of a victim of injustice."

"They could be responding to the death of that baby."

"But they always responded immediately," Daria said. "The baby died a week ago."

"They might have needed a week to plan this operation. Or they might have waited for the concert at the governor's house."

"But in their usual pattern the Cobras would have killed the plant manager, or they would have killed a politician. These guys are giving the government a chance to stop the injustice *before* they kill anyone."

"Maybe they've become more sophisticated."

"Yeah, maybe. But this operation has a serious flaw."

"What's the flaw?" Ronan asked.

"It depends on people reacting the way Ernesto wants them to. If the company doesn't tow the plant out to sea and sink it, then what remaining options does he have?"

"He can kill us, or he can let us go."

"If he lets us go, we can identify him."

"But that might not be a reason for killing us."

"Are you trying to believe he won't kill us?"

"I'm only trying to understand him," Ronan said. "As long as he has the governor he has a reason for killing us—to make them believe his threat to kill the governor. But without the governor we have no value as hostages."

"If we have no value, why wouldn't he kill us?"

"It wouldn't serve any purpose for him."

"It would eliminate three people who can identify him."

"Well, I don't think he's worried about being identified. They kidnapped us in front of hundreds of people, and they weren't wearing masks."

Daria considered. "If he's not worried about being identified, then he must have an exit strategy."

"He must have one. I don't think he's suicidal."

"I don't either. If he was, he would have snuck into the power plant with a bomb strapped to his chest."

"Yeah, that would have been easier than this operation."

The governor appeared, looking disheveled.

"Buenos días," Daria said. "I hope you like *mangú.*"

"Mangú?" the governor said as if he didn't know what it was.

"There's a pot on the stove. Help yourself."

The governor went over to the stove, peered into the pot, and made a face. "Is that all there is for breakfast?"

"I don't know. You could ask for room service."

Ignoring her, the governor got himself a mug of coffee and joined them at the table. After taking a cautious sip he said: "You know, you're not fooling me."

"What do you mean?" Daria asked.

"You're working with these guys."

"What makes you think that?"

"Your role was to talk with me and distract me," the governor said. "They didn't pick you out of the crowd randomly."

"They did. We don't know them, and we've never been in contact with them."

"Then how do you explain the fact that you were complaining to me about the power plant just a few minutes before they kidnapped us?"

"I was trying to make you aware of the fact that the plant is killing children in the *barrio.* But I didn't threaten to kill you."

"Well, these guys sent me a note threatening to kill me if I didn't make the company install filters."

"They wouldn't have threatened you," Daria said, "if the company *had* installed the filters."

Shaking his head, the governor said: "The plant is a pretext. This is really about politics."

"It's not about politics. It's about human lives."

"You don't understand. Whatever they call themselves, these guys are communists. They want to take over our government and turn us into another Cuba."

Ronan laughed. "You can't be serious."

"I am serious. And it's no laughing matter."

"I'm sorry, but if you paid attention to what they've been doing, you'd understand that they only want to stop injustices."

"That's what the communists say they want to do."

"That's what politicians say they want to do," Daria said, "including you. But you haven't done anything about the problems."

"We don't have the money," the governor said. "We're a poor country."

"We have the money for people like you to live in luxury. And don't tell me you bought that house on your government salary."

"I bought it with money I made in business."

"Well, I don't care about your house. I want you to order the power company to do what Ernesto says."

"So you *are* working with him."

"We're not working with him, but we have the same goal."

"I'm glad we have the same goal," Ernesto said, appearing. He looked as if he had gotten a good night's sleep. "Does that include you, governor?"

"You can stop the show," the governor said. "I know what's really happening?"

"You do? What's really happening?"

"These people are working with you. You're not going to kill them. You only want to make me think you're going to kill them."

"Do I have to kill one of them right now to convince you it's not a show?"

"Yes. Go ahead. I dare you."

Ernesto looked at him with contempt. "You know I'm capable of killing them, and yet you dare me to kill one of them?"

"I know you won't do it because they're working with you."

"You don't know shit. And you're willing to sacrifice one of them for nothing. That tells me a lot about you."

"It doesn't tell you anything about me—except that I can see through you."

"You can't see through yourself. You want to believe it's only a show so you can justify not doing anything to save them. Well, you better wake up. It's not a show. If the government doesn't do what I say, I'm going to start killing them, and if I have to kill one of them I'm going to kill you—painfully. *Entiendes?*"

The governor, pale, was speechless.

"I didn't hear you."

"Sí, lo entiendo."

"Then let me bring you all up to date," Ernesto said. "The acting governor has received our demand, so the clock is ticking. They have until Wednesday to start towing the plant away. If they haven't done anything by then, we're going to kill one of you, and we're going to deliver the body to them."

"Would it help if the governor ordered them to tow the plant away?" Daria asked.

"It might," Ernesto said. "But how would the governor order them to do it?"

"He could write a note to them."

"How would we deliver the note?"

"The same way you deliver the body."

Ernesto grimaced. "I'll think about it. How's the *mangú?*"

"It could use more onions," Daria said.

"And more butter," Filo said.

"You don't like *mangú?*" Ernesto asked the governor.

The governor mournfully shook his head.

Ronan was working on a master's degree in English at Fordham when he heard that Pat had been killed by the paramilitaries. A band of armed men had invaded his house and taken him out into the street and shot him as a warning to the people not to support the guerrillas. They trashed the house and set it on fire.

The news reached Ronan in a letter from a guy who had worked with him building schools. It recounted what had happened, and it enclosed a piece of cloth that was badly charred, a relic from the quilt with the letters l-i-b from the announcement: "The Lord sent me to bring glad tidings to the poor, to proclaim liberty to captives."

It was almost a year since Ronan had returned from Colombia, and not a single day had passed without his thinking about Pat, remembering how they worked together, how they talked with each other, and how the people revered the priest who lived among them in the *barrio*.

Over the next several weeks Ronan mourned for the person who meant more to him than anyone in the whole world, and by the end of that period he reached the logical outcome of the process—the decision to become a priest.

At the time he was living in an apartment in the Bronx within walking distance of Fordham, and he saw his family about once a month, usually on a Sunday after joining them for noon mass at St. Joseph's. After church they would have a traditional Sunday dinner, usually with the whole family present. His brother, now married, brought his wife to these dinners. She was quiet and polite and wise enough to stay out of the family discussions.

On the Sunday after he had enrolled in the seminary Ronan announced his decision to his family. They were at the table having dessert.

"What?" his father said in shock. "You did what?"

"I enrolled at Dunwoodie."

"Why on earth did you do that?"

"I want to be a priest."

"Since when?"

"I don't know. I guess I've been moving in that direction for the past several years."

"You were influenced by Father O'Shea?"

"I was greatly influenced by him."

"And you want to be like him?"

"Of course I do. I admire him more than anyone I ever knew."

"But you don't have to be a priest to be like him."

"I know," Ronan said, "but I want to be a priest like him."

"I think you want to escape from life."

"I don't want to escape from life. I want to continue Father O'Shea's mission."

"Did you talk with Father Scanlon about this?" Molly asked, referring to the local pastor.

"No. I made the decision myself."

"I think it would be helpful to talk with him. I mean, he went to the seminary, so he can tell you what it's like."

"Okay. I'll talk with him."

"To be a priest," his father said, "you need to have a calling. And I don't see that in you."

"If you don't see it, then you don't know me."

"I know you. You're my son."

"Well, I have a calling, and I'm going to pursue it."

"You have our blessing," Molly said before his father could say anything.

He looked at his father for confirmation.

"All right, all right. But if you ever have any doubts, you can change your mind—at least until you take your final vows."

The seminary was like college, except that its purpose was much clearer, and his four years there went by more quickly than his four years at Fordham.

When he completed the program he was assigned to a church in a poor area of the Bronx, and there he felt the kind of satisfaction he had felt in Colombia. By the end of six months he was sure that he had found his vocation, but before he was ordained he had to go through a rigorous self-examination as well as a session of intensive questioning by his mentor.

"You do understand," his mentor said, "that when you're ordained, it's final."

"I understand," Ronan said.

"We all have weaknesses, but do you have any particular weaknesses that would make you unfit to be a priest?"

"I don't know of any."

"What about sexual desires?"

"I haven't had any problem with them."

"What does that mean?"

"It means I haven't had any problem with them."

"Do you have them?"

"I have them, but they're under control."

"Have you ever acted on them?"

"No. I haven't," he said, remembering Amy and Lyle. "I've always controlled them."

"Even in high school?" his mentor asked skeptically.

"Even there. I never kissed a girl."

"Did you ever kiss a boy?"

"Of course not."

"Well, what if you had a strong sexual desire for one of your parishioners?"

"I hope I wouldn't, but if I did I would control it."

"What if it was overpowering?"

"I would pray to God for strength to control it."

His mentor nodded as if he was satisfied. "Do you have any other weaknesses that we should know about?"

"I have lapses in faith."

"Serious lapses?"

"They don't last long, but I have them now and then."

"We all have them. But if they don't last long, they're not serious."

A month later he was ordained at St. Patrick's cathedral, and he was assigned to the church of San Pedro in south Yonkers.

There wasn't enough water for them to take showers, so as the days passed they became grubby. The women adapted to the situation, tying their hair back and washing their underwear in the sink, but the governor complained about the lack of amenities.

"You should live in the *barrio*," Daria told him.

"I don't want to live in the *barrio*," the governor said. "And I don't want to live here. I want to live in my comfortable house."

Their conversations with the governor usually didn't get beyond such points. In fact, they preferred talking with Ernesto, with whom they had some common values. And on Monday evening after Ernesto had reported that the government hadn't taken any action, they talked with him in the kitchen without the governor being present.

"Did you manage to deliver a note from the governor?" Daria asked him.

"We did," Ernesto said. "But so far it hasn't had any effect."

"Are you surprised that they haven't done anything yet?"

"I am. I thought they'd want to save the governor."

"Maybe they want to get rid of him," Ronan suggested.

"Maybe they do. I just thought that for once they'd rise above politics."

"So if they don't do anything by Wednesday," Daria said, "you're going to start killing us?"

"I have to," Ernesto said. "I have no choice."

"You do have a choice. You could abandon this operation and find another way to achieve your goal."

"There isn't another way."

"There *is* another way," Daria said. "You could blow up the plant yourself."

"I thought of that, but I didn't want to leave a mess in the harbor."

"In that respect," Ronan said, "your plan is better than ours."

Ernesto frowned. "You had a plan to blow up the plant?"

"Yeah, we did," Daria said. "We sent a note to the governor threatening to kill a politician if he didn't make the plant install filters by September 10."

"If he hadn't met your deadline, would you have killed a politician?"

"No. We would have blown up the plant. The threat to kill a politician was only a ruse so they wouldn't increase security at the plant."

Ernesto considered, and then he shook his head, saying: "I don't believe it. You're just trying to make me feel you're on my side."

"We *are* on your side," Daria said. "I mean, we have the same goal. But we don't accept your method of achieving it."

"That's understandable. You want me to let you go."

"We want you to let us all go, including the governor."

"I'm going to let you all go," Ernesto said, "when they've done what I asked them to do."

"Then you must have an exit plan."

"I do. If I get word that they've towed the plant out to sea and sunk it, then we'll leave you all here, unharmed, and we'll get away. When we're safely across the border I'll call the police and tell them how to find you."

"You mean the border with Haiti?"

"It's the only border we have."

"Well, they'd have a hard time finding you there."

"I hope they would. But if they catch us and bring us back, I'm willing to do time in prison. It's a small price to pay for getting rid of that power plant."

Daria nodded as if she would be willing to pay the same price.

The next day passed without the government doing anything about the plant.

They were hoping that at this point Ernesto would abandon his plan and let them go, but after dinner he met with Daria, Filo, and Ronan and told them that by noon the next day they would have to decide which one of them he should kill first.

They decided to sleep on it.

TWELVE

RONAN LAY AWAKE most of the night thinking about the conversation that he would have with Daria and Filo in the morning. Without any question he knew the right thing for him to do, but he didn't know how to present it to them, so he played the conversation over and over in his head until he saw the first light of dawn through the barred window.

After another breakfast of *mangú* the guards left them alone in the sitting room so that they could talk. They sat in the armchairs as the guests of Rancho Escondido must have sat preparing for a day of hiking in the mountains.

"I should be the one," Filo said without any prompting. "I'm the least valuable of the three of us. For one thing, I can't have children."

"You *have* children," Daria said. "And what would happen to them without you?"

"They could find someone to take my place."

"They couldn't. There's no one who would love them the way you do."

"I agree," Ronan said.

"I should be the one," Daria said. "They could always find another doctor."

"No, they couldn't," Filo said. "There's no one who would care about the people in the *barrio* the way you do."

"I agree," Ronan said.

"Well, don't say you should be the one," Daria told him.

"I should be. I'm the least valuable. You both have missions, but I don't have a mission, and I don't have anyone who depends on me."

"I depend on you," Filo said.

"I do too," Daria said.

194

"You could find anyone to do your paperwork. You don't need me."

There was a silence.

"Why are we playing his game?" Daria asked.

"I don't know," Filo said. "Why are we?"

"Ernesto wants us to make the decision so he won't feel responsible. But what if we told him to make the decision?"

"It would make him stop and think."

"It could buy us time," Ronan said. "But I'm not going to let him pick one of you."

Daria looked around. "You know, this is the first time we've had a chance to talk without guards listening to us. So we should take advantage of it."

"How do you mean?" Filo asked.

"We should figure out how to escape from here."

"It wouldn't be easy to escape," Ronan said, "with four guys watching us."

"So how can we stop them from watching us?"

"By getting them to watch someone else."

"The only other person for them to watch is the governor."

"We can use him to create a diversion," Ronan said, thinking. "If we can get him to try to escape, they'll go after him."

"All four of them?"

"Yeah, maybe. The governor's the only hostage whose life has value. We're just extras."

"And if they lose him, the game's over," Daria said.

"But how can we get him to try to escape?" Filo asked.

"We make him believe they're about to kill him."

"How can we do that?"

"We tell him Ernesto has decided to abandon the operation, and he doesn't want to leave any witnesses."

"But why would he believe us? He thinks we're working with Ernesto."

"That's exactly why he *would* believe us," Ronan said.

"Then why would we warn him?"

"You're good people."

"What about you?"

"I shouldn't be the one who warns him."

"No, he wouldn't trust a *gringo*," Daria agreed.

"I'll do it," Filo said. "I think the governor likes me."

"When we have lunch," Ronan said, "you'll have a chance to talk with him, not at the table but at the stove. He doesn't eat the *mangú*, but he eats the rice and beans. So when he goes to help himself, go over to the stove and join him."

"How will he escape?" Daria asked.

"The last time I saw them, the keys were in the ignition of the jeep that brought us here, and they haven't used it, so they're probably still there."

"What if they're not?"

"Then he'll have to run."

"I wish we could use the other jeep. I won't be able to run in these shoes."

"I won't either," Filo said. "We should have worn sneakers to the governor's party."

"You'll have to go barefoot. There's no way that the three of us could get into a jeep before they stopped us. Or shot us," Ronan added.

"They wouldn't shoot the governor?"

"No. His life has value."

"How will he get out the door?" Daria asked.

"Before he sits down at the table," Ronan said, "he'll go to the bathroom to wash his hands as he always does. They've been letting him go there by himself. And from there he can walk to the door without being seen. They won't know where he went until they hear him start the jeep."

"And then they'll all run out after him?"

"I hope they will. They won't be thinking about us."

"Well, let's try it. We have nothing to lose."

They had just finished going over the plan when Ernesto appeared.

"Have you made a decision?" he asked them as if it was only a matter of what they would like to have for dinner.

"We have," Daria said. "We've decided to let you make the decision."

He frowned in disbelief. "You really want me to make it?"

"Yes. We think you'll make a better decision than we could."

"And what if you don't like my decision?"

"Whatever you decide, we won't like it. But there's nothing we can do about it."

"All right. I'll think about it," Ernesto said, "and I'll let you know by five this evening."

At least their tactic had bought them some time.

Ronan served for almost three years as assistant pastor at San Pedro. He should have been happy, but he wasn't. At the very beginning he discovered that he was unable to love the people of the parish, or he was unwilling to love them. He remembered what the Argentine priest had said, that sin was refusing to love, and it made him feel like a sinner. In fact, it made him feel like the ultimate sinner.

He was good at performing the functions of a priest, but increasingly he felt like he was only playing a role. Without love, he was a fake. And he prayed daily that God would enable him to love, or make him willing to love, or at least forgive his sin of refusing to love. But as time passed, his problem became less bearable.

The crisis occurred when a beautiful Latina woman started attending the mass in Spanish with her two children, a boy and a girl who he later learned were eight and nine. They dutifully followed their mother up the aisle to receive communion, both with such a strong resemblance to their mother that they couldn't have been anyone else's children. They weren't accompanied by a father, but that wasn't unusual. The fathers, who worked in construction or in restaurant kitchens, regarded Sunday as an opportunity to catch up on their sleep.

Shortly after he first noticed the woman at mass he saw her at an ESL class that the church offered on weekday evenings. He didn't teach in the program, but he was responsible for finding the teachers, who were mostly students in the education program at St. Catherine College, so he reviewed them periodically. On this particular evening he paused in his rounds to watch the woman ask for directions in English. Her eyes had a look of determination, and her mouth had a compelling allure. Perhaps aware that she was being watched, she turned toward him, and upon seeing him she clapped a hand over her mouth as if she had suddenly recognized him.

When the class was over he lingered in the hallway, waiting for her and wondering where she had seen him before.

"Father Ronan," she said as if she had witnessed a miracle. "My name is Yolanda, and I'm from a village near Popayán where you and Father O'Shea built a school. My husband worked with you, and I brought his dinner every day."

"Was his name Manuel?" he asked, remembering.

"That's right. He was very strong."

"He was a good worker."

"He was a good man."

"Why did you leave Colombia?"

"We left because they killed Manuel."

"I'm sorry," he said, conscious of the inadequacy of his response. "Who killed him?"

"The same people who killed Father O'Shea."

At a loss he could only ask: "Do you live in this area?"

"Yes. We share an apartment with my brother, who came here several years ago."

He imagined five or six of them all living in a one-bedroom apartment, as many of them did. "Do you have a job?"

"I clean houses. That's all I can do until I learn English."

"Well, if I can help you," he told her, "please let me know. I'm here for you."

"Thank you, father. I'll remember that."

A few weeks later she was in his office asking about the possibility of her children becoming altar servers. She had talked with them about it, and they liked the idea. After being uprooted from Colombia, they wanted to belong somewhere, and the church was a familiar place.

As they talked he was again conscious of the inadequacy of his response to this woman and her situation. He had multiple reasons for loving her, but he couldn't feel any love. He was only going through the motions of helping her. And he began to wonder if he really cared what happened to her.

When she had gone he went directly to a chapel and prayed. But it didn't help. It only made things worse because in praying he realized that he couldn't feel any love for God. He seemed to be incapable of feeling love.

In despair he remembered what St. John said: "Whoever is without love does not know God, for God is love."

After several days of mental agony he consulted his pastor, who listened to him patiently and then said: "Don't worry about it. We all have moments of doubt."

"But this isn't a moment of doubt. It's a void inside of me."

"There's no void inside of you. There's still love. You've just lost touch with it."

"I haven't just lost touch with it," Ronan said. "I've lost the ability to love because I refused to love people."

"Who did you refuse to love?"

"My brother, and my stepmother, and other people who wanted me to love them. They loved me, and I refused to love them back."

"You loved Father O'Shea."

"That was different."

"How was it different?"

"He didn't need my love."

"Okay." The pastor frowned. "And you think this woman from Colombia needs your love?"

"I think she does," Ronan said, "and for some reason I can't give it to her."

The pastor looked as if he was beginning to understand the situaation. "This woman is attractive. So maybe you have feelings of desire for her that have gotten in the way."

"That's not the problem. I mean, I'm aware of how attractive she is, but that should make it easier to love her, shouldn't it?"

"It should. It's easier to love attractive people."

"I think I know what the problem is."

"What's the problem?"

"I'm paying for my sin."

"What sin?" the pastor asked, looking concerned. The last thing he wanted to hear was that his assistant pastor was a pederast.

"Refusing to love."

The pastor looked immensely relieved. "Well, that's not the worst sin you could have committed, though it *is* a problem. Maybe you need to see a counselor."

"Maybe I need to take a leave of absence."

"That might be good for *you*, but it wouldn't be good for our church. You know we have a shortage of priests."

"But if I don't feel love for people," Ronan said, "then I can't function as a priest."

"Until now you've been functioning fine. But maybe you should take a vacation."

"I think I should take the summer off."

The pastor considered. "There might be a priest from Ghana available for the summer. I didn't put in a request for one, but I still might be able to get one."

"Please try to get one."

"Okay. I will. But if I can't get one," the pastor said. "I can't let you take the summer off. I can't do everything myself."

"I understand," Ronan said.

The pastor was able to get a priest from Ghana for the summer, and to show his gratitude Ronan asked his father to make a substantial contribution to San Pedro. His father was happy to do that, evidently hoping that if Ronan got away from the church for a while he might change his mind about being a priest.

Ronan lay on his bed, locked in his room, waiting for lunch and confronting the fact that by the end of the day he could be dead. He believed it wasn't an accident that he was in this situation.

Instead of dealing with his problem he had taken a leave of absence from it. But it had followed him to Santa Cruz, and he had been given a second chance with Daria and Filo and Elsa and Leticia. He had found the love inside of him by showing it through his actions. And maybe he would have one last chance of showing it.

He got out of bed and went to the window and looked out at the mountain and imagined Christ turning around and offering him a way to redeem himself. The vision wasn't clear since a cloud had drifted across the mountain, but he was alerted to watch for an opportunity. And he prayed for the courage to seize whatever opportunity might arise.

He was still at the window when he heard the knock on his door and the lock being opened. By the time he went out the guard was no longer in the hallway, and Ronan went by himself to the kitchen, where he found Daria, Filo, and Ernesto seated at the table. He helped himself to some chicken, rice, and beans, and he sat down with them.

The governor was the last to join them. He went to the stove and paused there for a while as if he were debating whether to eat this humble food.

"It's really good," Filo told him, going to the stove to get some more. She stood close to him and put a hand on his back affectionately.

"If you say so," he said, picking up a plate.

"I'll help you," she said, reaching for the serving spoon in the pot. She brought her face to his ear as she put a generous helping of rice onto his plate.

"The chicken is good," Daria told Ernesto, who was sitting next to her.

"I'm glad you like it," Ernesto said.

"Where did you get it?"

"From a nearby farm."

"I could tell it was fresh."

"It was walking around early this morning."

"Who killed it?" Daria asked.

"The farmer killed it. I don't like killing chickens."

"But you don't mind killing people?"

"I mind killing people," Ernesto said, "but I will if I have to."

"Has the government done anything yet?"

"It hadn't as of an hour ago. It has until five."

"Well, I'll keep praying that it does something."

"If I believed in God, I would too."

"You don't believe in God?"

Ernesto shook his head, saying: "How can I believe in a God who lets the smoke from that plant kill children?"

"That's a good question," Daria said. "But it sounds like you're blaming God for the plant, which suggests that you do believe in Him."

"I'm not blaming God. I'm blaming people who value money more than human life."

"But if you judge them, you should judge yourself for valuing social justice more than human life."

"There are times when we have to make sacrifices."

"So why don't you sacrifice yourself? Why don't you go on a hunger strike until they tow the plant away?"

"They wouldn't respond. They don't care if I live or die."

"I guess they don't," Daria admitted. "So it would be a waste to sacrifice yourself."

"It would be," Ernesto agreed.

"Well, they don't care if *we* live or die, so it would also be a waste to sacrifice us."

"If it is a waste, then I still have the governor."

At that moment the guy in question set his plate down on the table and said: "I have to go to the bathroom."

Ronan held his breath, praying that as usual they would let him go there by himself.

They did, being occupied with their food.

Filo sat down with another helping.

"You eat like a growing girl," Ernesto said, eyeing her.

"I'm feeding my soul," Filo said.

"These women are saints," Ronan said.

"They're certainly beautiful," Ernesto said.

"You know what happens to people who kill saints?"

"No. What happens to them?"

"They're hurled into the lowest circle of hell."

"If God will punish me for killing them, why won't He punish the owners of that plant for killing children?"

"He will in time."

"Well, that's not soon enough for me."

There was the sound of an engine starting in the carport.

"*Qué carajo?*" Ernesto said, jumping to his feet.

The four guys ran out of the kitchen, leaving the women and Ronan at the table.

"Come on," he said, knocking over his chair. He rushed toward the back door.

He led the women out onto a patio. It was grown over, and on the far side it merged with the forest.

Finding a path, he went into the forest with the women close behind him. They had ditched their high-heels and were running barefoot, keeping up with him.

Ronan thought they had gotten away when he heard Ernesto shout: "Stop!"

They stopped and turned around and were surprised to see Ernesto only about twenty feet behind them, pointing a pistol at them.

Behind him were the other three guys with pistols in hand.

If they had caught the governor they all wouldn't have been there, so Ronan knew that the governor had escaped.

"Come on," Ernesto said. "We're going back."

They had no choice, so they started walking slowly back to the house.

"Where's the governor?" Daria asked.

"He escaped, God damn it."

"Why didn't you follow him in the other jeep?"

"He took the keys. For a politician, he's pretty quick."

"Well, we have no value as hostages now."

"I know," Ernesto muttered as if he didn't appreciate her pointing that out.

"So you won't accomplish anything by killing one of us."

"Keep walking and stop talking."

Daria did stop talking, at least until they were back in the house, and then she said: "You have about a half hour before the army arrives."

"I know. You don't have to tell me."

"So you should get out of here while you can."

"And leave you here?"

"Well, we're no good as human shields. They'll shoot right through us, especially after the governor tells them we're working with you."

"I guess you're right." Ernesto turned to the other three guys. "We should get out of here while we can."

The guys didn't argue with him.

"Come on. Let's go."

Before they could move a voice from a megaphone boomed: "We have you surrounded. You can't escape. So lay down your weapons and come out with your hands raised."

"*Mierda!*" Ernesto said. "How the hell did they get here so fast?"

"They must have been in this area," Ronan said.

"They think we're the Cobras," the short guy said.

"You're not the Cobras?" Daria said.

"No. We're not," Ernesto said.

"Then who are you?"

"I'm the father of a baby who was killed by smoke from the power plant. And these guys are fathers of other children who were killed by the plant."

"I understand," Daria said, nodding sympathetically. "You had personal reasons for doing this."

"*Correcto.* We didn't have political reasons."

"So you weren't going to kill us."

"We never were. We only wanted them to believe we were going to kill you so that they would take us seriously."

"You have five minutes," the voice from the megaphone warned them. "If you don't come out with your hands raised, we're going to open fire on the house."

"If we go out they'll kill us," the tall guy said.

"If we stay here they'll kill us," the short guy said.

"If we try to escape they'll kill us," the other guy said.

"I think I have a way to save us," Ronan told them, seeing the opportunity that he had been watching for. "I'll go out and make peace with them."

"If you go out they'll kill you," the tall guy said, repeating his opinion.

"No, they won't," Ronan said on faith. He looked around for something to use as a white flag, but the only thing he saw was Filo's shirt. "Guys, turn your backs."

"Why?" Ernesto asked.

"Just do what I say. Filo, I need your shirt. I'll trade my shirt for it." He unbuttoned the *chacabana* he had bought for the governor's party and took it off.

Without asking for an explanation Filo took off her white shirt and handed it to him, taking his blue shirt and putting it on.

"It's the first time," Daria told her, "I've ever seen you in anything but white."

"Guys, you can turn around," Ronan told them. He got the broom and took off its head. Then he tied Filo's shirt onto it, one sleeve at the end and the other in the middle.

"You really think that'll stop them from killing you?" Ernesto asked cynically.

"I hope it will. I pray that it will."

"You don't have to do this," Daria said.

"Please don't," Filo said.

"They'll blow your head off," the tall guy said.

Ignoring them, he went to the door and opened it. He walked out with the flag raised and said with authority: *"Soy cura.* I am a priest."

BOOK CLUB GUIDE TO

Leave of Absence

Tom Milton

Introduction

Ronan Byrne has taken a leave of absence from his profession and has come to the Dominican Republic, where instead of finding peace in the coastal town of Santa Cruz he gets involved in conflicts over issues of social justice. Though he is the narrator, Ronan is an enigma. We learn that he is a high-school teacher, and at first he tells people he's on vacation, but then he admits that he's on a leave of absence because he had a career crisis. From the moment he arrives in Santa Cruz he feels at home among a group of expatriates who are said to be fugitives wanted by the law in their home countries. We wonder if Ronan is wanted by the law, and from his chronic feeling of guilt we infer that he has done something wrong. In periodic flashbacks we begin to understand him, but we still don't know exactly what he did.

He rents an apartment in Santa Cruz, and when he goes to the general store to buy provisions he meets Daria, a doctor who has a clinic in the *barrio*. She shows him how the unfiltered smoke from a power plant is driven by the prevailing wind into the *barrio*, where it is causing lung diseases, especially among children. She explains that the plant was brought to Santa Cruz by a foreign investor, who towed it from another country where it didn't meet environmental standards. For three years she has been trying to get the government to make the plant conform with the law and install filters, but the foreign investor has evidently paid off officials in order to avoid the expense of cleaning up the plant. For something to do, Ronan begins helping Daria in the back office of her clinic, doing paperwork so that she can report to her donors how she is using their money.

He also meets Filo, a close friend of Daria, who is operating a center to rehabilitate children who were victims of sex slavery. Filo is trying to get the government to shut down a hotel for sex tourism that is violating a number of laws, including the zoning law that does not permit hotels in a residential area and the law regarding the age of consent for sexual relations. But the foreign owners of the hotel have evidently paid off officials in order to avoid being shut down. To learn more about the hotel's operations, Ronan goes to its restaurant for a cup of coffee. There he is offered two girls who look like they are barely fourteen. After being tempted he rejects the offer and vows to rescue the two girls, who Filo says are sex slaves.

When the body of a girl who worked at the hotel is found on the beach, evidently killed by a sex tourist, the pace of action accelerates. The Cobras, a band of guerillas committed to social justice, randomly kills a sex tourist and hangs his mutilated body on the gate of the hotel as a warning to foreigners who exploit Dominican children. That action has the desired effect on the hotel's business, at least for a while, and as Daria and Filo become frustrated in their nonviolent efforts to get the government to take legal action against the power plant and the hotel, they wonder if violence is the only way to achieve their goals.

A conversation with Tom Milton

In this novel you pursue some issues that you addressed in previous novels, but I see at least one new issue: the exploitation of poor people in developing countries by foreign investors who care only about making money.

It's about time I got to that issue, especially since I spent a large part of my professional life arranging financing for development projects. I can't say that none of our projects had any negative effects, but at least we had a criterion that—assuming the project was economically viable—the effects should be beneficial to people. It wasn't all about making money.

You have two heroines in this novel, Daria and Filo, who have missions to oppose injustice and help its victims. In that sense they're like the heroines of your other novels. But as always you've created unique individuals, with their own histories and motivations, and while they're heroic they're also touchingly human.

They're based on women I've known and admired in the real world.

I noticed that after four consecutive novels told from a female point of view, this one is told from a male point of view, as your first four novels were. How do you decide which point of view to use in a novel?

When I want to show a heroine in action, I like to use the point of view of a male who admires or even loves her. When I want to emphasize the psychological development of a heroine, I like to use her point of view.

Unlike your other male narrators, this one is an enigma. I mean, we know that Ronan is a high-school teacher, but we don't know why he has taken a leave of absence. We soon learn that he had a career crisis, but we don't know what caused it. And from his chronic feeling of guilt, we infer that he has done something wrong. So this novel is as much about the narrator as it is about the heroines.

You're right. It's about how the narrator faces what he has done and tries to redeem himself.

In the flashbacks we gradually learn about him, while in the present we follow the development of his relationships with Daria and Filo, and we follow the events that move the story forward. As usual, you tell a fascinating story.

For me the purpose of a story is not only to engage the reader but also to reveal character and convey a message. So in my novels nothing happens by accident.

As we see Ronan getting involved with Daria and Filo we wonder if he'll commit himself fully to their missions, which make increasing demands on him.

The question is, will he overcome the fear that has held him back in the past?

You mean his fear of sharing his common humanity with other people.

Yes. The fear that makes him refuse to love.

I'd like to talk more about that, but I don't want to give too much away. So let's talk about the theme of violence. Like your other heroines who oppose injustice, both of these women are committed to nonviolence. But then they see how the Cobras, a band of guerrillas, are getting results by using violence, so they begin to wonder if the Cobras have the right idea.

That's why some people who are against using violence for political purposes eventually turn to it. They feel they're getting nowhere, and they begin to wonder if violence is the only way.

You showed that process in All the Flowers *when Teri is attracted to a band of urban guerrillas who have taken up arms against the government in order to end the Vietnam War. She begins to wonder if they have the right idea.*

It happens in many situations. It starts with a peaceful demonstration and when nothing changes it deteriorates into violence. We can see that process now in the Arab world, and we've seen it in Europe, Latin America, and our own country.

But once again I think you're saying that violence isn't the solution.

To quote a character from an earlier book: "Violence only leads to violence."

So is violence ever morally justified in achieving a goal?

I believe it's never morally justified. I also believe that people who use violence for political purposes can never achieve their goals. So there are both moral and practical reasons for not using violence for political purposes.

In this novel you again raise the issue of sex slavery, which was the main issue of Outside the Gate *and also an issue in* Infamy. *Why did you raise this issue again in* Leave of Absence?

I wanted to show it from another perspective. In *Outside the Gate* I show it from the perspective of a woman whose twelve-year-old daughter is kidnapped and sold into sex slavery. In *Leave of Absence* I show it from the perspective of a woman who was sold by her own mother into sex slavery and is now trying to help its victims.

I can understand why Ronan loves Daria and Filo. The guys who sit at the round table in Joop's Beach Bar regard these two women as saints, but they're more human than most of the saints that I remember. And I love the scene in the beauty shop when they do a makeover of Ronan.

I had a lot of fun writing that scene.

I also love the way you used the guys at the round table. Like Ronan, they're fugitives, so he can relate to them. And like a chorus in a Greek play they tell us about things that happen offstage and they comment on them. In addition, they give us a sense of the expatriate community in Santa Cruz, and they provide humor.

I also had a lot of fun writing those scenes.

I understand that you've spent a lot of time in the Dominican Republic, and that you even have a home there, so I have to assume that at least to some extent this novel is based on your experience there. But are you showing what it's really like there?

As in all my other settings, I'm showing what it's like beneath the surface. I'm showing what tourists or casual visitors don't see. That's why I write novels—to raise awareness of injustices that may lie beneath the surface.

Discussion questions

1. How does the author use flashbacks in this story?

2. Are there clues in the flashbacks that prepare us for learning what caused Ronan to have a career crisis?

3. How is the statue of Christ the Redeemer on top of the mountain used to reveal what is happening inside Ronan?

4. Daria and Filo have similar missions in that they are both trying to stop a project owned by foreign investors from hurting local people, but they have different challenges. Explain.

5. Do you believe that if all else failed, Daria would have carried out her plan to blow up the power plant?

6. Would Daria have been justified in blowing up the plant?

7. Is there any way that Daria and Filo could have joined forces with the Cobras without compromising their values?

8. Beyond what she has already done, what more do you think Filo could do to shut down Arabian Nights?

9. Would Ronan have had the same motivation to free the girls from Arabian Nights if he hadn't been tempted by Vilma's offer?

10. Do you think Daria and Filo were surprised to learn Ronan's identity at the end of the story?

11. What do you think happens to Ronan?

12. What role does Father O'Shea play in the story?

13. How does the character of Sergio, the police detective, evolve through the story?

14. How does the author use the guys sitting and drinking at the round table?

15. What particular role does Donal play in these scenes?

16. What techniques does the author use to create the setting of the story?

CPSIA information can be obtained at www.ICGtesting.com
Printed in the USA
BVOW03s2041260314

348890BV00001B/2/P